ROWDY'S RAIDERS

Hearing of the murder of his step-mother and attacks on the Triple Creek ranch, Rowdy Carter gave up his life as leader of the Raiders to come home and defend the ranch. The mighty Lazy K spread is behind the attacks, but when its gunmen prove no match for the ex-leader of the elite of the Confederate Cavalry, renegades are hired. Triple Creek is captured and Rowdy's step-sister kidnapped. Rowdy cannot strike back alone, so he reforms the Raiders . . .

EDWIN DEREK

ROWDY'S RAIDERS

Complete and Unabridged

LINFORD
Leicester

First published in Great Britain in 1996 by
Robert Hale Limited
London

First Linford Edition
published 1997
by arrangement with
Robert Hale Limited
London

British Library CIP Data

Derek, Edwin
　　Rowdy's raiders.—Large print ed.—
Linford western library
　　1. Western stories
　　2. Large type books
　　I. Title
　　823.9′14 [F]

ISBN 0–7089–5131–7

Published by
F. A. Thorpe (Publishing) Ltd.
Anstey, Leicestershire
Set by Words & Graphics Ltd.
Anstey, Leicestershire
Printed and bound in Great Britain by
T. J. International Ltd., Padstow, Cornwall

This book is printed on acid-free paper

1

AS he drifted quietly into Clearwater he surveyed the scene, his face reflecting his distaste at what he saw. It didn't feel like coming home at all, he might just as well be drifting into yet another town. The two saloons his father had once forbidden him to enter had been replaced by one mighty saloon-cum-whorehouse. In front of its red doorway women openly plied their trade, the oldest profession in the world. The main street, once full of pleasant folk chitter-chattering about their daily life, was now full of gun-toting vermin, two of whom eyed the drifter with considerable distaste.

Though he looked the part, dressed in an old and ragged uniform of the Confederacy, he was most certainly not an ordinary drifter. It was a letter, not chance, that had caused him to return home after so many years. He rode on a huge black stallion, built for power not looks. A careful study of the rig on the back of the stallion would have revealed that it was a most unusual and expensive saddle, part Texan, part Mexican design. From its large front pommel hung two holsters, each of which appeared to contain a six-gun. The drifter did not tote a gun, but behind him in the superb Texicana saddle hung two shoulder weapons. To his left, a deadly Spencer repeating carbine. On his right a double-barrelled shotgun. Made in England and of exquisite quality, the very high value of the shotgun indicated that the drifter was a man of considerable wealth in spite of his ragged appearance.

A pack-mule laden with bulging saddle-bags trotted alongside the big black stallion. An immaculate Henry repeating rifle was draped across the back of the mule. The Henry was a rare and much sought after weapon, easily the best rifle used during the Civil War. Only about 7,000 of them had been supplied and those solely to the Union. No, armed with only the best, this man was no ordinary drifter as the two gunmen should have realized.

Unfortunately for them, the two failed to notice either the unusual saddle or the arms the drifter carried. They were distracted by the arrival of an old and battered chuck-wagon driven by an equally old and battered-looking Indian. The chuck-wagon was loaded with furniture and pulled up outside the hardware store. In spite of his advancing years the Indian began to unload the wagon and carry the furniture into the store. No one offered to help though several able-bodied young men passed nearby. None of them were prepared to risk the wrath of the two gunmen.

The drifter watched the old Indian but he too did not offer to help. He remembered how proud the Indian had once been. Instead he picked up one of the saddle-bags and headed to the bank, leaving his weapons behind. The gunmen watched him for a moment then turned away. Unarmed, the drifter posed little threat to them. They continued to watch the Indian as he struggled to unload the wagon. They had no intention of preventing the Indian from unloading, nor would they interfere so long as he left with an empty wagon. Loading it with provisions for the Triple Creek ranch was another matter. They had instructions to do anything they thought necessary to prevent that from happening. However, without help it was clear that it would be some time before the Indian finished unloading, so although it was still early, the two gunmen strutted over to the whorehouse where they were at once surrounded by the women of that establishment.

At first the travel-stained drifter was not well received in the bank. He asked to see the manager, but was kept waiting for several minutes before

4

a wizened bank teller, old before his time, finally attended him. Even then the teller addressed the drifter as if he were a simpleton.

"Our manager, Mr Reno, is a busy man. He only sees important clients, like Major Norton of the Lazy K, without an appointment."

"He will see me," said the man staring hard at the teller.

The teller blinked and wilted under the steady gaze of the drifter. There was something in his eyes that told the teller that here was a man used to giving orders and having them obeyed. He appeared to be a man who had ridden to Hell yet somehow had survived the experience. Without another word, the teller left the counter and hurried to the manager's office. He was so disturbed by the drifter's piercing stare that he forgot to knock on the mahogany door.

The teller was almost right about the drifter: he had ridden around a living Hell and survived. Not once but twice. He was one of the few who had ridden with the great Jeb Stuart, leader of the Confederate Cavalry, on both epic rides completely around General McClellan's mighty Union Army of the Potomac. Outnumbered by a hundred to one they had twice inflicted heavy casualties on the enemy as well as gathering vital intelligence and valuable supplies.

They made Stuart a general for the first circumnavigation of the Army of the Potomac and the young drifter got his first stripe. He got his second when Jeb Stuart did it again, successfully riding behind the same mighty Yankee army causing mayhem and chaos. The drifter grinned to himself at the memory. 1500 Confederate Cavalry against an army of 134,000. Yet they had lost only three men and captured vast quantities of horses and arms, again gathering invaluable intelligence. No wonder Abraham Lincoln had sacked General McClellan. Yet that had been only the beginning of the legend of Jeb

Stuart, and the drifter had played his part in most of Stuart's many daring raids. However, such daring couldn't last. The drifter lost touch with Stuart after the general became Lee's right-hand man. This followed the tragic death of 'Stonewall' Jackson, killed by one of his own sentries. Stuart had seemed invincible yet he too was killed. With the death of these two great generals, died the hopes of the South.

He had served under General Nathan B Forrest after that. The general had asked for him specially, such had been his growing reputation. Forrest had been one of the South's greatest military tacticians but he had been intensely disliked by many influential Confederate leaders, possibly because alone of the South's leading generals he had been directly involved in the slave trade. Or perhaps it was because he was the only senior ranking officer in the entire Southern cavalry who had not been to West Point.

Perhaps that was the reason for Forrest personally granting the drifter, then only a sergeant, a commission. But Forrest's involvement with slavery and his fanatical hatred of Negroes, especially those who carried arms, was too much for the drifter to stomach. Even so he had learned much from that flawed genius whom many leading Union generals regarded as their most dangerous adversary.

So, after he had recovered from a wound, caused not by the enemy but an over-zealous Confederate sentry, the drifter had joined Mosby's Confederacy or the 43rd Virginian Irregulars as they were more properly known. He became a fully fledged captain only to find that rank signified little in the Irregulars. Only ability commanded respect. But ability he had in plenty and he saw out the Civil War fighting guerrilla style. Mosby's men supplied themselves entirely from their foraging raids against the Yankees. Anything captured from the Union Army such as guns, ammunition, food and, not least, money, was kept by his men. However, unlike Quantrill's Marauders they did not prey on civilians, and protected Virginia as best they could. Nor did they kill Negroes as General Forrest's cavalry had done.

Though he fought for the South, the drifter's views on slavery coincided with the Unionists. During the Civil War he had learned much about real life and even more about the art of killing. So when the war ended there was much call for the services of a man who had fought with such distinction.

He was brought abruptly to the present by the return of the wizened bank teller. A few minutes later he finally found himself in the manager's office. Seated behind a vast wooden desk was a portly man dressed in a crimson-coloured, velvet jacket, white lace shirt and matching cravat. Black riding breeches and boots completed his outfit. The man would have looked more at home on one of the gambling ships of the Mississippi than in a respectable bank. His name was Barnabus Reno. No one was allowed to call him Barney. He looked at the drifter as if he were a leper. Finally he spoke to him.

"Now what can I do for you, Mr er . . . er? I'm afraid I didn't catch your name."

"Carter, I'm here to pay off the Triple Creek mortgage and claim my father's ranch back."

If Barnabus Reno was surprised he didn't show it.

"So you're Rod Carter. Well young Rod, I hardly think you'd have the money to do that."

Barnabus Reno was a self-made man with a dubious past, but it didn't stop him brimming with self-conceit and arrogance. As he looked at the ragged uniform of the former Confederate cavalryman he made little effort to hide his contempt or to control the sneer on his face.

Without a word Rod Carter flung

open the saddle-bag he was carrying, then tipped the contents on to the desk. Thousands of gold coins clattered noisily on to the hard black top. They almost covered its entire surface. The gold coins were part of the spoils he had gained while serving with Mosby.

"That enough?"

"Are they real?" gasped Reno.

"A lot of men died for nothing if they are not, but you can get them assayed if you wish."

"No, that won't be necessary," the bank manager replied, "but see here Mr Carter, there's clearly more than enough to pay off the mortgage completely."

"Do so, then open an account for me with the rest." Rod Carter, as the bank manager had called him, almost spat out the words.

"Certainly," said Barnabus Reno, his manner changed to a fawning one by the gold on his desk. "Is there anything else I can do for you?"

"Yes, tell Major Norton of the

Lazy K to get any of their cattle off my land. One week, no more, then any steers on my land become mine. Tell them that and make sure they know I mean it."

"Mr Carter, you will start another range war."

"No, just finish the last one," said the drifter as he walked out of the office.

No one came to help the old Indian as he single-handedly unloaded the goods from the wagon and carted them into the store. No one offered to help him as he reloaded the chuck-wagon with much needed provisions for the Triple Creek ranch. No one came to his aid when the two gunmen, finished with the floozies in the whorehouse, began to tip out the provisions from the newly loaded chuck-wagon. No one helped as the two gunmen savagely beat the old Indian when he tried to stop them. No one, even though several scurried by the helpless old man, as he cried out in pain. They knew better than to tangle with the hired gunmen of the Lazy K.

No one came to the old Indian's aid until the drifter came out of the bank. He walked slowly in order to go unnoticed as he was unarmed. When he reached the big black stallion he grabbed his Spencer carbine and fired a warning shot which missed the first gunman by barely a whisker.

With the instinct of a natural killer, the first gunman span round firing his Colt revolver as he did so. But the .44 bullet of the Army Colt hit the dirt of the street, falling well short of his intended target. The second gunman realizing he too was out of range, threw down his Colt. Then he raised his hands, cursing loudly at his stupidity in underestimating the drifter. His fellow gunman realizing that they were in a no-win situation against the Spencer carbine also dropped his Colt and raised his hands.

"You all right, Kital, Son of Prancing Bear?" called out the drifter in the dialect of the Running Dog tribe.

"Old Kital will live to scalp these sons of whores," cursed the old Indian.

"Easy my old friend," replied the drifter, still in the Indian's own language. "I have a much better idea."

He turned to face the bewildered gunmen, neither of whom had understood his conversation with Kital.

"Take off your boots and drop your pants," he ordered.

The two gunmen hesitated. A second and third bullet from the drifter's carbine landed only fractionally away from each of the gunmen's boots covering them with street dirt. The rapidity of fire from the Spencer left the men in no doubt that the drifter was using one of the new repeating carbines. Hastily they complied, much to the amusement of the gathering crowd. In a few moments the two gunmen stood by the pile of their discarded clothes, motionless with arms raised. Barefoot and clad only in their pink long-johns they were subject to much ridicule from the large crowd.

"Now you can reload the chuckwagon," said the drifter.

It was early afternoon and the overhead sun blazed down on to the dusty street. In spite of wearing only their pink long-johns the two men sweated profusely. Soon they began to hobble as the hot and stony street took its toll on the bare soles of their feet. Eventually they finished the job and the wagon was ready to leave. The drifter pointed to their horses, still tethered to the saloon rail. Very gingerly the two picked their way across Clearwater's main street.

"On your horses and take this message back to the Lazy K," ordered the drifter. "Anyone who thinks that the Triple Creek is an easy target has to deal with me first. When you've delivered the message, ride on and don't return. This is the first time in six years I've not killed the person I was aiming at."

But they didn't heed the warning. Red-faced with embarrassment, they mounted their horses painfully, groaning out aloud as the stirrups cut into their unprotected feet. Both knew that they must return to Clearwater and kill the drifter in order to save face. Word of what he had done to them would spread like wildfire. They would become the subject of many bawdy jokes. Who then would employ them as gunmen? It never occurred to them the drifter expected his warning to be ignored.

Nor did it occur to them to check out the second stranger to arrive in Clearwater that day. He was tall, lean and dressed totally in black. The second stranger remained on horseback by the bank, his hawk-like eyes never leaving the drifter, his hand poised only inches from his Remington six-gun. The stranger had met the drifter once before, but although they had both fought on the same side during the war, there the similarity ended.

The stranger was a wanted criminal, an outlaw with a high price for his capture, dead or alive.

Only once did the merest hint of a smile briefly flicker across the otherwise emotionless face of the stranger as the two gunmen were forced to disrobe. Then he turned his grey mare around and rode slowly away, so as not to attract attention. Even then, his hand was still positioned directly over his Remington pistol. The attention of the crowd was fully focused on the two hapless gunmen as the stranger rode slowly away, although the drifter's ugly black stallion noticed the pretty grey mare as it left. Black Bart could do nothing but whinny in frustration since it and the pack-mule were still tethered to the bank rail.

"Are you all right?" the drifter asked the old Indian, but this time in English.

If the Indian recognized him he gave no sign of doing so.

"Sure, be even better when I'm out of this damned town. You'd better be gone too, the law don't like anyone who upsets Lazy K hands. That ain't surprising considering that's where they get their pay," replied Kital, also in English.

"What happened to Sheriff Lattimer?" asked the drifter.

The Indian climbed unsteadily on to the old chuck-wagon, shaking his head sorrowfully as he did so. Without uttering a word he urged the horses on and the wagon moved forward leaving a cloud of swirling dust in its wake. As it lumbered on its way, a series of groans and creaks came from its heavily laden body. The old wagon had been badly neglected for a long time. Rod Carter wondered whether the rest of the Triple Creek ranch had been as badly neglected as he walked into the store.

It had changed little since his boyhood days. Everything was piled high in untidy heaps, from picks and shovels to dress material; from building material to grain. Guns and

18

ammunition of all types could be purchased from the store. If they hadn't got it then the James family would get it. Anything and everything except for barbed-wire, strictly forbidden on the open ranges that surrounded Clearwater. As in the past, everything lay strewn haphazardly across the floor. It was all still here just as it had been in the days of his childhood. However, he was disappointed to see that the James family no longer ran the store.

"Made bad enemies there," said the storekeeper grimly.

He was a large, balding, middle-aged man, once well built but now more than a little overweight. Like the store he now ran, his appearance was untidy yet there was something about him that indicated that he would not be pushed around.

"Those two ain't much; they got took too easily. Have you got any .42 calibre shells?" asked the drifter, changing the subject.

"There's not just those two gunmen

at the Lazy K, though they are bad enough. Some of them ain't too particular how they earn their money, so watch your back," said the storekeeper. "Now, you did say .42 calibre, didn't you? Well now, it's a long time since I sold any of that. Still, there might be a box out the back somewhere. Tell me what you got that uses that size of bullet?"

The drifter was not prepared to reveal that they were for a very special and unusual two-barrelled revolver used only by a very few Confederate officers. The Le Mat was a French design and had been made to a unique specification. Not only were the two barrels of different calibre but they were mounted on top of each other, not side by side as in a shotgun. The Le Mat had more than once saved his life but its effectiveness lay in keeping its special features secret. His own gun bore a special mark which indicated that it had actually been made in England, probably by the

Birmingham Small Arms Company. It had been manufactured to a far higher specification than those made in France and consequently far superior to its French counterparts.

"Opening a furniture store?" he asked, not wishing to discuss the Le Mat with the storekeeper.

"Not really. The bank says I can't give Triple Creek any more credit, and the Lazy K backs the bank with its gunmen," said the storekeeper.

"So how come you got the furniture?"

"Nobody said I couldn't trade with them," laughed the storekeeper. "Besides, I figure that little gal needs all the help she can get, on account of old Carter being near killed in the raid. They did for her mother, you know."

Rod Carter felt a cold rage consume him, as he heard what had happened to his father. The letter that had been passed on to him by General Mosby had told of the death of his stepmother but this was the first news he had had about his father. The girl mentioned by the storekeeper must be his stepsister, Dawn. He couldn't imagine her running the Triple Creek ranch. Perhaps she had mellowed as she had grown older, though she couldn't be much more than nineteen.

"How much for the furniture?" he asked.

"Couldn't sell it, friend. No offence intended, but I am going to store it until the Triple Creek can afford to get it back," said the storekeeper.

"No offence taken," Rod replied, as he placed a pile of coins on the counter. "This enough to take care of the Triple Creek debt?"

"Sure is, but you don't have to, friend. A little on account will be fine, pay the rest when you can."

"Seems that not all the newcomers to Clearwater are so bad," he said, smiling. "Better you take it all now. From what you say about the Lazy K gunmen, I might be a bad risk."

"There's still far too much," protested the storekeeper.

"Use some of it to pay for the furniture to get back to Triple Creek. Hire me a wagon and a driver," said the drifter.

"You can use my old wagon, I'll load it myself after I've closed. I'll leave it round the back for you. Nobody is going to risk driving it to Triple Creek in case they run into any Lazy K gunmen," replied the storekeeper.

"Then I'll have to drive it. Put in a few boxes of shells for the Henry and my Spencer. They were, well let's say, borrowed from the Union so it's .58 calibre I want, not Confederate size."

"Got plenty and .577 if ever you want them. One day you must tell me how you came by the Henry, not even Major Norton's got one of those beauties," said the storekeeper.

"Sure, but not today, it's too long a story," said the drifter.

He smiled as he recalled how he had captured the Henry rifle from the Union camp at Occuquan. That had been during the Dumfries Raid back in the Christmas of '62. It seemed a lifetime ago.

"Another time, perhaps. Any one against the Lazy K is welcome here," said the portly storekeeper.

"I'll look forward to telling you the story one day soon. In the meantime should there be any trouble over hiring out your wagon, tell the Lazy K to deal with me. Tell them I won't be hard to find, Mr Storekeeper."

2

THE great black stallion, less than pleased to have suffered the indignity of being hitched to the bank rail, eyed his master with much displeasure. Then it issued a snort of pure disgust because it was not allowed to follow the tracks of the young grey mare it had met earlier that day. Instead it was forced to go in the opposite direction towards the little side street where Sheriff Lattimer and his daughter used to live. The pack-mule, uncomplaining as ever, followed dutifully behind.

It was only the shortest of rides down the main street to the small block of houses where the Lattimers lived. Yet once a cavalry man, always a cavalry man; the habit of riding everywhere was now second nature to him. At this end of town nothing seemed to

25

have changed. Even the spring blooms in the well-kept gardens seemed the same as when he was a boy.

He dismounted and opened the white picket gate he had opened so many times as a lad. His father and the sheriff had formed a deep friendship during the Mexican War and, as a boy, he had gladly taken any message his father wanted to send to the sheriff. In those halcyon, far-off days of his youth, he had always fancied the sheriff's daughter, Anne Lattimer. Tongue-tied by youthful innocence, he had never been able to do anything about it. Clever, pretty and a year or so older than himself, Anne had always been the most sought after girl in the town. She had seemed out of reach of a boy from a small ranch, although she had always been quite friendly. Now Anne must be twenty-seven, no doubt married, with a brood of children.

He knocked on the front door lightly. A cowboy in Yankee infantry uniform but wearing a ten-gallon hat came to the door. He wore his two Colts with their butts pointing forward, slung low from his hips. Rod began to regret that he had left his own handguns on his horse.

"What do you want, Reb?" the cowboy snarled.

"Does Sheriff Lattimer still live here?" he asked politely, remembering that he was unarmed.

"What's that to a Johnny Reb? Clear off!" came the angry retort.

So saying the cowboy drew both guns and fired them into the ground inches from Rod's feet. The .44 bullets ricocheted off the stone path dangerously close to his feet. However, unlike the two gunmen a few minutes earlier, Rod neither flinched nor moved. He simply repeated the question.

"Does Sheriff Lattimer live here?"

"Looks like you can't take a hint, Reb. You ain't wanted here," growled the cowboy.

"Rex, that's enough of that," said a cultured, feminine voice from inside the house. "This is still my father's house and we will see who we like."

"Just as you say, Anne," said the cowboy ungraciously as he holstered his handguns. "Anyway I've got to get back to the ranch with your father's reply. Major Norton ain't going to like it, not one bit. You'd better start being extra nice to me, gal, and then I might put in a good word, make the major go a bit easier on you when he gets back from the cattle drive."

"Good afternoon, Rex, I'll see you when the major returns," the feminine voice said coldly from inside the house.

"As for you, Johnny Reb, this has been your lucky day," said the cowboy. "I hate all rebs, but right now I got a job to do. So get out of town, then you can tell people that you crossed Rex Morden's path and lived to tell the tale. If you're still here when I get back with Major Norton's reply, I'll kill you, armed or not."

So saying the cowboy stomped angrily down the path as the owner of the cultured, feminine voice came to the door. All thoughts of Rex Morden disappeared from his mind as Anne smiled at him. She was dressed in a simple, tight-fitting white dress which almost touched the ground. Her long black hair was curled into a bun. He glanced at her left hand; surprisingly she was not wearing a ring of any sort. For a moment he reverted to being the tongue-tied callow youth who had scarcely dared speak to her. Then she spoke, in that soft voice he had almost forgotten. The gentleness of her voice broke the spell. After the carnage he had gone through, and the many women he had known, nothing could shake him, or so he had thought. But now in front of Anne he was not so sure.

"Can I help you? I'm afraid my father is no longer the sheriff."

"Come now, Anne, surely you recognize me?" he said gently. "Once this was almost my second home. I hope I'm still welcome?"

For a second Anne looked startled

then recognition shone in her eyes. She threw herself into his arms and kissed him passionately until he began to feel that he was no longer a drifter. They were interrupted by Anne's father who came to the door to see what all the commotion was about.

"What's going on here?" he asked.

Rod extricated himself from Anne's embrace as quickly as he could, his face flushed with embarrassment. Once again he imagined himself as a young teenager about to be severely lectured by the town sheriff. Once again the feeling left as soon as it had come, this time driven out by an ice-cold rage, for where Bill Lattimer's right hand had once been there was nothing but an empty sleeve. No wonder he was no longer sheriff. Bill Lattimer's right hand, his gun hand, had been amputated just above his wrist.

"Look who it is, Daddy, it's Rod Carter," said Anne excitedly.

"I know who it is," said her father sharply. "Don't be a stranger, young man; come in and tell me your news, it's been a long time since you left. It's good to see you again, there's been little to cheer about for long enough."

It was the second time that day he had been called Rod. He had not been called that since he had left home and joined the Confederacy. The great Jeb Stuart thought Rod sounded too much like a Yankee name and had given him a nickname that had stuck with him throughout the Civil War. But the war was long over and the use of his Christian name made it feel more like coming home. Anne ushered him in to the parlour where he was invited to sit on the couch in spite of his grimy clothes. Bill Lattimer sat down in the armchair nearest the unlit fire.

Anne sat down, but not on the couch beside him. Then she never had when he was a boy. In their youth she had always chosen to be, well, if not quite aloof then just out of reach. Now, to his great surprise, she sat down on his knees and put her arms around him tightly. It was as if they had been much closer than just childhood friends. She did not seem to mind that his trail-begrimed uniform dirtied her pretty white dress. The feeling of coming home was getting stronger and much to his surprise he discovered that he liked it.

After a few minutes of general gossip her father beckoned to Anne. She got up rather reluctantly and went into the kitchen. As she did so, he noticed that her once crisp white dress bore stains caused by close contact with his grubby uniform.

"You will stay to dinner, won't you, Rod? Anne will never forgive me if you don't," said Bill Lattimer.

"Love to, sir, but I have to look after my horses first," he replied, finally remembering his cavalry training.

"Take them into the paddock behind the house," said the former sheriff. "You can leave your saddle in the outhouse if you like, your things will be safe enough there."

The black stallion took one look at the long, lush grass of the paddock and decided that it was for him. When his master unsaddled both him and the mule, the stallion almost forgave him for not following the grey mare.

It took him the best part of thirty minutes to unsaddle both horse and mule and to put his belongings in the outhouse. Both the large Texicana saddle and the saddle-bags were heavy and he had to make several trips. The saddle-bags contained the rest of his money but it was the Henry rifle, and the English double-barrelled shotgun that he took into the Lattimers' house.

As he walked into the kitchen he was met by the delicious smell of stew as it bubbled on the kitchen stove. He had not eaten that day, nothing unusual for a one-time member of the Confederate cavalry, but he had become soft fighting with Mosby's Irregulars and now missing meals came hard. There was barely time for a quick wash before he was summoned into the parlour to eat.

Anne had somehow managed to find time to cook dinner and change into a soft-blue dress. It had a beguiling neckline which more than hinted how generously nature had endowed her with feminine charms. It seemed to Rod that Anne was much changed from the cold and aloof girl of his boyhood. This was one of the few changes in Clearwater of which he approved.

Anne insisted on clearing up after dinner, leaving Rod alone with her father. The former sheriff studied Rod's Henry rifle and shotgun with undisguised admiration. He then went to the bureau which he unlocked with some difficulty. He had only his left hand to use so it was only after a great struggle that he opened the top drawer. Triumphantly he pulled out a revolver and offered it to the man he knew as Rod Carter. Bill Lattimer was still a proud man and did not ask for help, so none was offered.

"Man I took this off said it was the best ever made. Didn't do him any good though, someone shot him in the back," said Bill.

The young Carter gently removed the pistol from its holster and spun the handgun on his finger. It was beautifully balanced. It was neither a Colt nor a Remington pistol, nor was it a Confederate copy of either of them. Indeed, it was a make he had never seen before. That was surprising for he had been on many successful raids with Stuart, Forrest and Mosby. During these raids large quantities of Union weapons, many imported from Europe, had been captured. However, the handgun was not like any of them. Reluctantly he returned the gun to its holster and put it down on the dinner-table.

"Got you guessing, my boy," laughed Bill Lattimer. "It's a Whitney Second Model. It uses .36 calibre shells like any old Navy model but has almost as much stopping power as the normal Army .44."

"Does it shoot as well as it feels?"

"Only if you're good with a handgun, my boy. You see I never got the chance to use it because of this," said the sheriff holding up his handless right arm. "So tell me, how good are you? The truth now Rod, more than your life rides on your answer."

"Accurate and pretty quick, sir," replied Rod, quietly realizing that this was not the time for false modesty.

"How quick, young man?" asked Bill Lattimer.

"There's faster. Met one once, said he rode for Quantrill's Marauders. Absolute lightning he was. Funny, he seemed a decent sort, but then perhaps not all that has been said against Quantrill is true."

"Don't bet on it, Rod. War brings the scum to the surface no matter which side. Did this man have a name, like Howard by any chance?" asked the old sheriff quietly.

"I didn't ask him, sir. At the time it seemed healthier not to."

"Quite right. Sometimes that sort of

information can be bad for your health. Here take the gun, my boy, I can't use it but watch out for Rex Morden. That man is mean but unlike most bullies fears no man. Anyway, better change the subject. I can hear Anne coming back."

Anne entered carrying a tray full of steaming coffee cups. Rod hastily moved the Whitney on to the floor as she put the tray on the table and sat down close beside him. They talked of this and that as they recalled their childhood. So much did they enjoy themselves that the time flew by and soon it was evening. He knew it was time to move on, to collect the wagonload of furniture from the store and head for the Triple Creek ranch. However, he did not want to leave.

It had been several years since he left Triple Creek. Since then he had always been on the move, after all it was the cavalry he had joined. Until now he had always enjoyed moving around, but now, he wished he could stay. Anne pouted and seemed displeased when he explained about the wagon waiting to be picked up so, seeing his daughter's disappointment, Bill Lattimer gave him the excuse to stay a little longer. He took it gladly without really knowing why. Perhaps it was the warm welcome and the homely atmosphere or perhaps there was more to it than that? He didn't know.

"Why don't you stay here for the night? Then you could make a start before sun-up," suggested the ex-sheriff of Clearwater.

"You can sleep on the couch," interrupted Anne eagerly.

"Better to arrive at Triple Creek in daylight when they can see you," continued Bill. "They are bound to be jumpy after today's episode at the store and we don't want them mistaking you for the Lazy K, do we? Accidents can happen in the dark you know."

Bill Lattimer was right. Rod remembered how he had once been wounded by a jumpy Confederate sentry. He also remembered that the second-in-command of the Confederate Army, General Stonewall Jackson had died after one of his sentries had inadvertently shot him. So Rod decided to wait until morning, but he could not leave the horse and wagon behind the store. However, Bill had anticipated the problem.

"Why don't you bring the wagon into the paddock?" he asked. "You could unhitch the horse and leave it to graze with the others."

Rod agreed and went to collect it immediately. Though it went against his cavalry training, he walked to the store. No point in incurring the wrath of his stallion for such a short journey. Sometimes he wondered who was master of whom where that animal was concerned.

It didn't take that long to walk to the store. True to his word, the storekeeper had left a fully loaded wagon at the back of the store. He drove it into the paddock, unhitched the horse and returned to the house. His black stallion remained at the far side of the paddock ignoring him and the storekeeper's old horse completely.

When he finally returned to the house he was surprised to find that Bill Lattimer had gone to bed leaving his daughter to keep him company. Anne had changed again and was now wearing a daring pink nightgown with an even lower neckline than her blue dress. This time she sat down beside him on the couch.

"Are you here to stay or will you be off again without a word to me like you did last time?" she asked.

"Well, I can't stay for long even though I want to, but I won't go until I've sorted things out here."

"What can you do, ranch boy, against the whole of the Lazy K?"

Anne had used the name she had always used in their childhood and he had always hated. It stung him into a response he instantly regretted, but he could not take the words back.

"I'm not the useless lad you used to know," he replied angrily. "War changed all that and everything about me, even my name. I'll get things straight at my father's ranch and in town before I have to leave."

"Sssh! Of course I know that, my ranch boy," Anne said tenderly. "I know all about you, your father brought me the clippings from the Richmond papers. Look I'll show you."

Anne went to her father's bureau and opened the second drawer. From it she brought a newspaper clipping. There was a picture of Rod Carter and General Stuart surrounded by the society ladies of Richmond. The caption read that a certain 'Rowdy' Carter was receiving a special bravery award from General Jeb Stuart. The article went on in great detail about Rowdy's military career and some of the battles in which he had fought. It also mentioned that he had enlisted as a trooper and had risen to sergeant in only a year. Worse still, the article called him by the nickname of Rowdy, first bestowed on him by General Jeb Stuart, the nickname by which he had become famous or notorious depending on the side for which you had fought.

"Yes, I know that you're not what you seem," said Anne softly. "I know they called you Rowdy. Dad knows, and your father knows that you are the famous, some folks round here might say infamous, Rowdy Carter. We know that you were the leader of the Raiders who fought for General Mosby."

But she only knew a part of it and Rowdy Carter, now on extended leave from the new United States cavalry, was not going to tell her the rest. Nor was he going to tell her of his time with the Texas Rangers. It was while working under cover for them after the end of the Civil War that he had picked up his second nickname of the drifter. Neither was he prepared to show Anne his letter of authority which carried the signature of the great Phil Sheridan, no less. That great man, once his deadly enemy, had personally sought him out and offered him a new commission. Now he was a major no less. He had come a long way since he had run away from home because of the amorous advances of his step-mother. Far enough to know when not to reveal the secrets of his past and present life.

Anne sat down beside him again and cuddled him amorously. Rowdy was at a loss to explain her behaviour, remembering how she had treated him with such disdain before he left Clearwater all those years ago. Not that he was complaining, it was like a dream come true.

"Last time you left so suddenly I didn't get chance to say goodbye," she said so softly he could hardly hear. "So this is more in the way of a welcome home present and something to bring you back to me when you have to leave again."

So saying she put her arms round him and kissed him with a passion that

Rowdy had seldom encountered. She did not object when he returned the kiss with interest. Nor did she object when her nightgown slipped down to her waist and she seemed more than happy to let it remain there. But Rowdy was a guest in the house of a man he had always respected. Bill Lattimer had left him alone with his daughter on trust and he could not break that trust in spite of his feelings. So while he still had a little self-control left, he gently pulled the sleeves of the nightgown back on to Anne's shoulders. However, only after a considerable delay. He was only human after all, no matter how good his intentions. Anne pouted in feigned annoyance, yet elation overrode her feelings of frustration.

* * *

Jack Denton paused to mop his brow and swat away the flies. The owner of the Running Dog ranch surveyed the mighty herd. Formed by the amalgamation of his steers with those of the Lazy K, the herd stretched as far as the eye could see. It had been a long hard drive and there was still some way to go before they reached Dodge.

Jack Denton had been astonished when Major Norton had suggested that the two ranches should combine their herds and forge a new cattle trail to Dodge. There had been open warfare between the two ranches for several years and at first Jack suspected the major's motives. However, the usual spring floods from the Indian Mountains had not happened. The Running Dog ranch relied on the overflow from Bottom Creek during spring to fill up its main lake. For some reason this year it had not happened. Without water, Jack was faced with losing his herd during the long, hot, dry summer.

So in spite of his doubts Jack had agreed to the drive. In truth the water shortage meant that he had little option. As a safeguard,

Jack insisted that the hands from the two ranches camped separately each night. However, although there had been ample opportunity for the major to doublecross him, so far nothing untoward had happened. Indeed, whenever the major visited the Running Dog camp he came unarmed. He also insisted that all his men remained unarmed, except when they rode point or were scouting the trail ahead, a condition he did not seek to impose on the cowhands of the Running Dog.

As the crow flies, Dodge was barely 500 miles north-west of Clearwater. Unfortunately, that route took them across the Wastelands. As yet the Wastelands had not been officially incorporated into the United States and therefore not yet patrolled by the cavalry. Not surprisingly the area had become a haven for outlaws, renegades and rustlers. As a result, driving a large herd across the Wastelands was out of the question.

To the north of Clearwater lay the

impenetrable Indian Mountains, so they had little choice but to embark on a long detour around them. At first the herd had gone eastwards for almost 200 miles until it reached the Arkansas river. Then the herd had turned north, following the river until it reached Fort Smith. At the fort a few hundred head of cattle had been sold to the army to pay for new provisions.

That had happened several days ago and the herd had continued to follow the river. It would do so for another hundred miles or so before turning due west and at last heading directly for Dodge. It was a long way round but unfortunately the outlaws that roamed the Wastelands and the Indian Mountains made the detour necessary. However, the grazing had been good and losses minimal. Indeed, the steers were heavier now than when they set out. They should certainly fetch a good price from the buyer that Major Norton promised would be eagerly waiting for them when they finally reached Dodge.

3

DAWN was just breaking as Rowdy Carter approached his old home, the Triple Creek ranch. Before crossing one of the creeks from which the ranch derived its name, he paused to look at the ranch. Strangely there was no sign of activity from the bunkhouse or the main building; strange, because on almost every ranch, the working day began at dawn.

As the sun rose its rays began to pierce the early morning spring mist as it hung above the tree-covered hills behind the ranch. Although it was a beautiful sight the signs of neglect were only too evident, even from a distance. The corral fence was broken in several places, not that it really mattered, there were no horses to be seen. The once immaculate yard between the bunkhouse and the main ranch house was untidy and far from clean. The little cottage garden at the side of the house had once been his father's pride and joy, now it looked sadly neglected. Feelings of guilt for staying away so long hit him hard. It was time to come home to stay; yet Rowdy knew that was still not possible. Perhaps it would never be.

The horse pulling the storekeeper's wagon took the opportunity to drink from the creek. It had taken two hours of steady climbing from the town to reach the Triple Creek ranch situated as it was near the foothills of the Indian Mountains. The old horse was well past its prime and not used to early morning work. While Rowdy waited he thought over the events of last night. Anne had grown into the lovely woman he had always imagined. However, he had never imagined that her welcome would be so warm. Yet what were her real feelings towards him? After all the years he had spent away from home, her passion had taken him completely by surprise.

Rowdy's thoughts were interrupted by a group of riders rapidly approaching from the opposite side of the ranch. They raced towards the house, guns drawn. If they saw the wagon, then they ignored it. Rowdy could see by their haste that they were intent on surprising the occupants of the ranch, a surprise that was not intended to be pleasant. The riders maintained their gallop right up to the front door, suddenly pulled up and began to fire their pistols into the air.

Startled by the sudden commotion, a young woman hurried out of the ranch house. Her red hair shone in the early morning sunlight but Rowdy did not recognize her. The horsemen stopped firing. Still mounted on their horses they began talking to the girl. It was obvious from the raised tone of their voices that the riders were far from friendly. However, Rowdy was too far away to make out what was being said.

Rowdy eased the wagon slowly forward out of the creek. If the riders noticed, they again paid no attention to it. They were all too busy arguing with the young woman. The redhead seemed to notice Rowdy and the wagon. Even from that distance, Rowdy could see hope glimmer in her eyes. The hope lasted for a second, then it was gone as she failed to recognize him.

Grabbing his doubled-barrelled shotgun, Rowdy was able to jump off the slowly moving wagon undetected by the four riders as it passed behind the bunkhouse. The old horse ambled slowly onwards, occasionally slowing still further to nibble the tender shoots of newly sprouting spring grass.

Rowdy quietly crept round the bunkhouse. Putting the early morning sun behind him, he approached the horsemen from the rear. He paused, hidden behind the wall, waiting for the wagon to arrive and distract the riders. It didn't, the horse had stopped to nibble a clump of tasty grass.

While he waited, Rowdy loaded his shotgun with buckshot. Buckshot was heavy so he carried only enough for one load. There would be no second chance if he got it wrong. Next he drew the Whitney pistol Bill Lattimer had given him the previous night and checked it carefully. How he wished there had been time to test it. He returned it to his holster. As he crept nearer, he began to make out the conversation.

"Give it up now. Look at the place, it's about to fall to bits."

It was one of the horsemen evidently speaking to the girl, but crouched behind the bunkhouse wall Rowdy could not tell which gunman was doing the talking.

"Never," came the defiant voice of the girl. "Anyway, if you hadn't chased our hands away the ranch wouldn't look so bad."

"Thought that would have been enough to show you that we mean business and you'd have the sense to sell to the Lazy K," came another voice.

"Seems not," came a third voice. "Seems we are going to have to convince you a bit more. Strip!"

"What!" gasped the girl.

"Strip or I'll work your old man over again. Only this time I won't stop at putting him in bed, I'll put him in a coffin," said the first voice.

From around the corner Rowdy heard the girl sob. Then all went quiet. Rowdy went white with anger as he heard what had happened to his father, but he forced himself to stay calm. A rash move now would only serve to get himself killed.

Rowdy risked cocking the shotgun as a roar of approval came from the horsemen. He could only assume that the girl had started to remove her clothes. Still, that might provide the distraction he had hoped to achieve by the appearance of the driverless wagon. Yet Rowdy continued to wait, hoping the girl was still disrobing. The more she took off the more the horsemen would be distracted. Against four he would need all the help he could get.

Rowdy took a deep breath to steady his nerves, then stepped round the corner of the bunkhouse. All four riders were still mounted. They didn't see him as they were too busy ogling the redheaded girl. Reluctantly, she undid the top of her short underbodice, the lower part of which barely covered her thighs. From her anguished expression, it was clear she wore nothing else beneath it.

The riders were intent on watching the actions of the half-naked woman. Indeed, a troop of raw cadets could have ridden up, bugles blowing, without them noticing. Rowdy, on the other hand, had spent most of the Civil War making lightning raids under Jeb Stuart or leading guerrilla attacks under Mosby. Experience had taught him how to turn situations like this to his advantage. Even so he could not bring himself to shoot the riders in the back. However, he was not about to get himself killed by any false sense of chivalry.

Rowdy pointed the double-barrelled shotgun at the feet of the four riders' horses and fired the first barrel. Buckshot ricocheted against the hooves of the startled horses. Dust flew skyward as the terrified horses bucked and jumped wildly, crashing into each other in their panic. Rowdy fired the second barrel into the air, barely above the heads of the four riders as they tried desperately to control their rearing mounts.

Unlike the Union Cavalry, shotguns had been used by many in the Confederacy during the Civil War. Rowdy had never used a sabre believing that if an enemy was near enough to use a sabre on him, that enemy was too damned close! He had always preferred the panic that buckshot caused when fired from close range.

Once again his idea had worked. Those riders not thrown to the ground by their wildly bucking horses dived to the ground to avoid the buckshot from the second barrel, the half-naked woman quite forgotten. All was confusion; rolling bodies, cries of pain and lurid curses filled the air. The kicking horses threw up great clouds of dust. Suddenly the unmounted horses shied away and bolted towards the shallow creek. They galloped through it at full speed, their hooves kicking up plumes of white foam. They galloped on and on, until they were out of sight.

Rowdy threw the empty shotgun to the ground and drew his Whitney. Less than a minute had elapsed since he had attacked the four as they ogled the half-naked redhead. Now, one lay prone in the dust knocked unconscious by a whirling hoof, another lay moaning as he nursed a broken arm, a third staggered up only to be confronted by Rowdy's drawn six-gun. All fight knocked out of him, he raised his hands high in token of abject surrender.

Not so the fourth rider. He had

landed unharmed, if undignified, on all fours. In a flash he leapt to his feet, drawing his Army Colt as he did so. Only a select few of the fastest gunslingers could outshoot a drawn pistol when in the hands of an expert. Too late the fourth gunman found out he did not belong to that elite band. Not that the information was any use to him because he was dead before he hit the ground, struck in the heart by Rowdy's only shot. The Whitney not only felt good to handle, it shot dead true, something that could not always be said for the Colt, many of which had been copied and mass-produced by other lesser manufacturers.

"Where the hell did you come from?" said the only uninjured rider, still keeping his hands high in the air.

"You might have come quicker, or did you want to get an eyeful too?" said the redhead who seemed more angry than grateful at Rowdy's intervention.

"He used you as a distraction and it

worked too," said the uninjured rider disgustedly.

The girl bent down and began to retrieve her clothes. She was still clad in the short bodice, the front of which was still half unbuttoned. As she bent forward, Rowdy could see that her breasts were delightfully freckled. Hastily, he looked away. The third rider was slowly beginning to recover consciousness. For the moment neither he, nor the rider with the broken arm, posed a threat. However, he couldn't watch all three of them at the same time.

"Will you get their guns?" he asked the young woman.

"Certainly. Then I can shoot the bastards," the woman replied.

"Go round behind them, don't get between them and me," said Rowdy.

"What sort of idiot do you think I am?" she retorted.

It was clear to Rowdy that the woman's temper was as fiery as the colour of her hair. In spite of himself he couldn't help noticing how attractive she was as she began to collect the guns. Although low-cut dresses had been the fashion for some time, the display of ankles, never mind legs, was considered very common. Yet there was nothing common about the exquisitely proportioned legs now on display before him. Rarely had he seen such an attractive sight.

While she collected the guns, Rowdy pondered what to do with the prisoners. During the Civil War, prisoners had often been unofficially exchanged, but the Lazy K had nothing he wanted. Sometimes prisoners had been set free, yet that would be taken as a sign of weakness by the Lazy K. Twice during the war he had seen prisoners shot in cold blood but he knew he couldn't do that. Even so he had to demonstrate that he was a power to be respected.

The girl had collected the riders' guns and dropped them down by Rowdy's side, then stooped and picked up the rest of her clothing. Seeing her half naked gave Rowdy the answer to his problem. He was going to serve out a little poetic justice and let her decide how far it should go. This time he would go further than he had done with the two gunmen in Clearwater.

"Strip," he said to the riders, and then spoke to the girl, "Want to get some lamp oil and something to light it with?"

Her face lit up as she saw what Rowdy had in mind. By the time she returned, the riders had removed everything bar their long-johns. These were red unlike the pink ones worn by the two town gunmen. With great relish the girl poured the lamp oil over the clothes and set them alight.

"Is that far enough for you?" Rowdy asked the girl.

"No, make them strip all the way," she replied.

"You heard the lady," laughed Rowdy, but there was no sign of mirth in his cold blue eyes, only death.

Five minutes later all three riders stood naked as they watched the last of their clothes go up in flames. If the sight of three naked men bothered or embarrassed the young woman in any way, she gave no sign. Instead she watched them walk very slowly away. Rowdy followed them as far as the storekeeper's wagon. Its old horse still contentedly munched grass, quite unmoved by all the noise and fuss caused by the gunshots. Nor had it responded to the other horses as they galloped past it.

Rowdy also watched the three naked men as they painfully made their way to the creek. They paddled across its shallow waters, cursing and swearing revenge as their feet encountered the stony bottom. They faced a long and embarrassing walk, unless their horses had stopped along the trail to feed.

Rowdy knew they would not forgive him for their humiliation. He knew they would be back. Like the two gunmen in town yesterday, they had to come back and face him to regain their reputation. In less than twenty-four hours he had antagonized several gunmen and Rex Morden. Not really the quiet return he had so carefully planned.

The Lazy K would make a formidable enemy and would soon come in force to catch him. However, there was nothing new in that. Whilst serving with Mosby he had been sought by General Custer's cavalry on the orders of the great Sheridan himself. Rowdy had outwitted them all and lived to tell the tale. It was strange that General Sheridan, once his most deadly enemy, was now his commanding officer. Such were the fortunes of war, for those lucky enough to survive it.

After the men had finally disappeared from view, Rowdy drove the wagon up to the front of the ranch house and began unloading the furniture. It was a heavy and tiring job. His respect for the old Indian grew immensely. Old Kital had also unloaded the furniture unaided. It took him an hour to unload the wagon. He had just finished when the woman returned. She had washed, combed her long red hair, put on Levis and a white shirt. Yet the masculine clothes only served to enhance her femininity.

"You'd better come in and have coffee," she said. Her voice was far from friendly and she showed little gratitude for his aid.

"I'll rustle up some breakfast if you like. Then you can tell me why you helped me and how you got my furniture back."

"Let me wash up first. I'll use the bunkhouse shower," replied Rowdy.

He turned away before she could answer. Without looking he walked directly towards the old shower. There was something in his walk that reminded the girl of someone from her past. Then it struck her, how did he know about the shower? It had not been used these many years, hardly at all since . . . No, it couldn't be, could it? Not him, not after all these years.

She raced to the same vantage point that her dead mother had used to spy on the young Rod Carter over six years ago. However, this time he removed only his Whitney and its holster. He showered with his clothes on. Not because of any false modesty, but simply to remove the trail grime and horse smell from his ragged clothes, the clothes he had chosen to wear when he played the part of the drifter, as an undercover agent for the Texas Rangers.

From her vantage point inside the ranch house, she watched him intently. She didn't know whether she was pleased or disappointed that he kept his clothes on. By the time he finished she knew that he was no ordinary drifter. She also knew why he had helped. The knowledge did not make her happy, far from it. He was the last person she wanted to feel indebted to and the last person she would have wanted to see her half naked.

By the time he had finished showering, the spring day had become quite warm. While he waited for his clothes to dry, Rowdy unhitched the old horse from the storekeeper's wagon and led it into the corral by the side of the old barn. He had to hobble the horse to prevent it from straying through the broken corral fencing. From the length of the grass in the corral it was clear that the storekeeper's old horse was the first to stay there for a long time. Everywhere he looked, the ranch appeared neglected. He had been away for far too long, the feelings of guilt almost overwhelmed him. There was much to be done before the summons came that would take him away again.

At the other side of the corral was the old barn. It had always been the last thing to be repaired on the ranch even when he was a boy. Now it was a virtual ruin and needed a lot more than a coat of paint to restore it. However, it was just the place to hide the ammunition, which was still in the wagon. He had bought plenty from the storekeeper except for the unusual .42 calibre used by his Le Mat special revolver. There was just one box of that calibre.

By the time he had completed the task to his satisfaction, his clothes were almost dry. The smell of bacon sizzling on top of the big range met him as he walked into the kitchen. Nothing seemed to have changed since his boyhood years and it reminded him of times long gone by. Yet Rowdy felt alone and uneasy. He felt like the prodigal son at last returning home. Late, but better late than never.

"So you've come home at last, Rod Carter," said the redhead as she entered the kitchen from the main room. "Well, I'm afraid you're too late on both counts."

Taken by surprise by the use of his name by an apparent stranger, Rowdy said nothing. He stared long and hard at her. In spite of her manly clothes there was no denying her natural girlish beauty. He found her very attractive, despite the waspishness of her tongue.

"Don't stand there with your tongue hanging out to dry. Sit down and I'll get you breakfast. I suppose you've earned it," she said sharply.

Only by her acid tones did Rowdy at last recognize her. It was Dawn, his once hated and feared little stepsister. She had grown into a young woman of great beauty, but her mean tongue, once experienced could never be forgotten. Once, in his long forgotten boyhood, that sharp vitriolic tongue would have lashed him without mercy. In those far-off days he became tongue-tied and embarrassed, so he could not respond. Yet that was an age ago. Now he was another person living another life, his youthful innocence long since gone. After experiencing the war, he no longer had any problems in facing Dawn.

"I'm surprised that you stayed at the ranch," he said, as he sat down to eat breakfast.

"This is my home now. Nobody is

going to take it away from me. Not the Lazy K, not the bank nor anyone else," replied Dawn looking hard at her stepbrother.

"Of course, if that's how you feel, then so be it," said Rowdy calmly, as he continued to eat the fried bacon and eggs.

"You'd better believe it, ranch boy!" said Dawn as she flounced angrily out of the kitchen.

It was the second time he had been called by his hated childhood nickname in the last twenty-four hours and again it got to him. As in his boyhood days, Dawn had gone before he could retort; like the old days, she had got in the last hurtful dig.

Dawn returned just as he finished breakfast. She had changed again, this time into riding clothes. She now wore a black leather jacket and a black riding skirt with matching black boots. She had tucked her long red hair under a black stetson. Her white blouse was primly laced up to her neck by a black leather thong. She smiled at him, yet there was a hint of sadness in her face.

"I'll take you to see your father if you wish, I've horses saddled up outside," she said quietly.

"Is he all right?"

"Stepbrother, I think that you should judge that for yourself when you see him."

"Where is he, Dawn?"

"With Kital in the Indian Mountains."

She had saddled up a horse for him as well as her own pinto. They rode across the range and up into the foothills where he had once roamed as a boy. As they reached the beginning of the beeline the going became steeper and much harder to ride. Yet Dawn rode the difficult terrain with the ease of one born to the trail. He remembered that before he left Triple Creek, the young Dawn would not even ride a horse, claiming it was much too undignified for a Southern lady. As he rode, Rowdy again looked hard and long at Dawn.

69

He liked what he saw, it seemed that his little brat of a stepsister had done a lot of growing up.

"You don't like what you see?" asked Dawn, blushing as she became aware of his gaze.

"Sorry, I didn't mean to stare. You didn't used to ride at all. Now you do it very well."

"Things change in six years. I hope that you have too, Rod."

"Was I that bad, Dawn?"

"Worse; you were a spoilt, uncouth brat, but then I don't suppose I was much better," she replied.

He didn't answer her as they entered a clearing. In the centre was a small pool. They dismounted to rest the horses and let them drink. While the horses were drinking, Dawn walked along the bank gazing wistfully into the pool. Rowdy followed, feeling more than a little awkward. This pool had once been his favourite place, his own haven from the outside world. Now he felt like an intruder in someone

70

else's private world. Far from feeling at home, he felt more like a drifter than ever.

"You were supposed to disagree with me back there," she said, still looking into the pool. "I'd hoped you would say that I wasn't that bad. I'd hoped stopping here would bring back some good memories for you."

"Ghosts more like," he replied, "but it was a nice idea and I thank you. It can't be easy for you, me turning up the way I did."

"Rod Carter, you've apologized to me and thanked me all in the space of a few minutes. I can't get used to you coming home and being nice to me all in one go." She laughed as she spoke, but there were large tears in her green eyes.

"Not my home any more, it's yours now. I'm not back for good, but you can bet I'm going to put a few things right before I have to go away again," he said bitterly.

She turned and walked back slowly

towards the horses. As she did so, she brushed past him and slightly overbalanced. He caught her gently and supported her. It seemed perfectly natural for them to continue walking slowly, arm in arm.

"Our father is not the man you remember," Dawn said slowly, choosing her words with care.

"I don't understand you," he said.

"They worked him over real bad. When Kital returned last night, he told me about the trouble he had in town, but not who you were. He and I must have words about that!" she said indignantly.

"Go on," encouraged Rowdy.

"After Kital told me about the trouble in Clearwater, I sent them both into the Indian Mountains. We are the only white folk who ever go there, so I thought they would be safe from the Lazy K," she replied.

"Leaving yourself on your own to fend them off."

His respect for his stepsister increased

and it showed. She coloured slightly and slipped out of his arms before replying. He was surprised by how much he had enjoyed having Dawn so close to him, even though she was his stepsister.

"There's no other way to say this to you, Rod. Father did everything he could to keep the ranch going after you left. All during the war he did the work of two men. Then, when it was all over, the range war started and they killed my mom. He seemed to lose heart after that. He needs all the good news he can get."

"It's a bit late. When I was needed most I was miles away, doing my own thing. After the war had finished I should have come back here and helped out," said Rowdy bitterly.

"What difference could you have made?" said Dawn angrily, as she mounted her pinto.

"Maybe none, but I should have been here anyway," he replied.

"Maybe, but you weren't. Anyway,

Father will be pleased to see you. He's very weak so don't go upsetting him by saying that you're going to be leaving again soon," Dawn said crossly and galloped away before Rowdy had time to remount his horse.

It took him almost ten minutes to catch up with her as she galloped up the mounting track. Although he was on a strange horse Rowdy had been riding since he had been able to walk. His natural riding ability had been honed to perfection by the training he had received in the cavalry. There, he had been considered to be amongst the best. Yet it took him all his time to catch up Dawn. Never once did she falter as she twisted and turned her pinto through the gullies and trees that led to the sacred burial grounds of the Running Dog Indians.

Rowdy could only marvel at Dawn's riding skill. She seemed perfectly at one with her pinto. Except for her waspish tongue, she seemed to have completely changed from the little brat who once claimed that true Southern ladies rode only in carriages or side-saddle. Strangely, he now found her quick temper fascinating and no longer hurtful. As he thought over the changes, he realized that Dawn's Southern drawl had completely vanished, another reason why he had initially failed to recognize her.

Suddenly she slowed to a walking pace and they rode silently together up a steep incline until they reached a small thickly wooded plateau. After another five minutes they came to a small clearing behind which towered the main heights of the Indian Mountains. In the centre of the clearing and in front of a series of caves was a medicine man in all his ceremonial regalia. It was Kital, Son of Prancing Bear, the last great chief of the Running Dog Indians. Shaking his head sadly, the old Indian beckoned the two riders to dismount.

"Bad times for you, worse times for old Kital," he said in perfect English.

"How's Father?" asked Dawn anxiously.

"Very weak. He will survive, now that he has hope," replied Kital. "This old Indian hasn't lost all his magic, but a visit from his children will work even greater wonders. Come Morning Sky, true daughter to my honoured enemy. You too, Master Rod. I have prepared the way and now your father is expecting you. He is still very weak. You may only stay for a very few minutes."

Rowdy thought the Indian name for Dawn delightful, although he was surprised at her calm acceptance of it. More and more, he saw that she was far removed from the spoilt Southern belle he once thought her to be. Had his boyhood judgement been that faulty? Perhaps he had been blinded by jealousy of her relationship with his father? After what had happened between him and Dawn's mother he suddenly felt appalled by his previous attitude towards her.

As they walked to the cave he had mixed feelings. How would his father react after all these years? His stepmother's highly passionate advances towards him, which he had returned with the full vigour of youth, had been reason enough for him to leave Triple Creek. Yet his father must never know the truth about his adulterous second wife. So how could he ever tell his father the real reason for his sudden departure all those years ago? So Rowdy hesitated as Dawn ran to the side of the frail old man lying on a bed of animal skins. She knelt down and gently hugged him. Rowdy was shocked to see how frail his father had become. It was plain to see the bond of deep affection between Dawn and his father. He felt ashamed. His was the blood relationship, not Dawn's. Yet in spite of that, she had proved to be a better daughter than he had been a son.

As if reading his thoughts, Dawn stood up and took him gently by the hand. Her face softened, or perhaps it was just a trick of the candlelight? Yet her hand somehow seemed reassuring as she led him to his father.

"Look who has come to see you, Father," she said in the gentlest of voices.

"Hello, Dad. I hope you're glad to see me," said Rowdy anxiously.

"Of course I am, Son. Welcome home, such as is left of it. If it hadn't been for Dawn, you would have nothing to come home to at all."

John Carter's voice was so weak that Rowdy had to bend down to hear him. Dawn was touched to see the two of them united again and discreetly moved away. Seeing her move away, John Carter whispered to his son, "If I don't recover, or if anything happens to me, promise that you will take care of Dawn."

"Of course, Dad. But Kital tells me that you're going to recover. I've paid off the bank, so everything is going to be fine."

"Perhaps. It's just a feeling I have, Son. I can't explain it."

"All right, Dad. If it makes you feel any better, I promise that I will look after Dawn as best as I can. In any case she will always have a home at Triple Creek for as long as she wants to call it home."

"Fine, Son. Now there's something I must tell you about her mother and me," continued Rowdy's father, his voice becoming weaker than ever.

Whether it was the effort of talking, the excitement of seeing his son again or what he was about to say to him, Kital couldn't tell. However, he could tell that John Carter was exhausted and in urgent need of rest. So he moved closer to his one-time enemy and laid a restraining hand on his shoulder.

"Enough, old man, you must rest and save your strength," said Kital.

As Kital ushered both Dawn and Rowdy out of the cave, Rowdy became increasingly concerned about his father.

"How come he's so weak?" he asked.

"They didn't just beat him up," said Dawn bitterly.

"No, they took him from the ranch and kept him without food for three weeks. Only then did they beat him up," said Kital.

"Why?" asked Rowdy.

"To make him sign over the water-rights of the ranch," replied Dawn. "They let him go because he was no use to them dead. Anyway the round-up was finished. Major Norton and most of his backshooters have gone on the cattle-drive. Gone to Dodge taking with him John Denton and the Running Dog herd."

"How many men left on the Lazy K?" asked Rowdy.

"Eight at the ranch, a few more in town," replied Kital.

"Don't forget the new sheriff and deputy. They're just two more of Norton's hirelings," said Dawn.

They spoke little on the ride back to Triple Creek. Dawn seemed both preoccupied and self-conscious while Rowdy had a lot to think over. Clearly he could not handle the Lazy K and the refurbishment of Triple Creek on his own. Nor could he expect any help from the meagre resources of the US Cavalry; that had been made clear to him before he took his leave of absence. So he was going to have to fight fire with fire, using the one resource he had in plenty. Although he had paid off the mortgage and debts of Triple Creek, he still had one saddle-bag filled with gold coins. Unlike most, he had done well out of the Civil War and had kept it.

Restoration of Triple Creek posed little problem. Even if the locals were intimidated by the Lazy K gunhands, there were always plenty of drifters willing to earn a few dollars before moving on to the next town. Men he could trust, capable of defending Triple Creek against the hired gunhawks of the Lazy K, were not so easy to come by. To find them he would almost certainly have to leave Clearwater.

Dodge was the obvious place. Since the railroad had reached it, Dodge had become a centre for cattle drives and a mecca for all who wished to deprive the drovers of their hard-earned money. Gambling tables and whorehouse girls filled its saloons. Rival gangs had several times tried to prevent the Texas herds from reaching the railhead.

Dodge had all the ingredients for a range war. Its towns folk needed it to stay wide open to attract the trail herds; on the other hand, the surrounding land was beginning to attract farmers. The last thing they needed were thousands of steers trampling all over their crops. For the moment the trail drivers had the upper hand, but for how long? Rowdy had no idea who would eventually win. However, he did know that such conditions would draw the best gunmen, like moths round a flame. Rowdy needed the best to defend Triple Creek.

Unfortunately, Major Norton was already well on his way to Dodge. No doubt the major had already sent men ahead into Dodge to hire gunmen to protect the herd as it crossed the farmlands. It was essential that Major Norton learnt nothing about Rowdy's plans to recruit gunmen until he had enough to defend Triple Creek. So Dodge was out of the question.

Abilene was another trail town with problems similar to Dodge, making it the next best place to recruit gunmen. Unfortunately, it was much further away. In any case he had to report back to his unit in Richmond to officially receive his new commission and his new uniform. Rowdy had little doubt that his leave of absence would be extended, but he would have to apply for the extension in person. While he was in Richmond he could try to recruit men capable of defending Triple Creek. It was a long shot but it was the best chance they had.

Even on a good horse like Black Bart, it would take many days' hard riding to reach Richmond. Once there he still had to find the right men to recruit. All that would take valuable time and by now Major Norton would be well on his way to Dodge with the herd. Even allowing for delays caused by the traditional celebrations after selling the herd, Major Norton and his hired cronies should be back in Clearwater before Rowdy could return with any recruits.

How to protect Dawn and Triple Creek while he was away? That was the real problem. His father should be relatively safe in the Indian Mountains. Protected by Kital, Dawn would also be safe there. However vulnerable the old medicine man might be in Clearwater, he was still more than a match for any amount of white men in his own sacred hills. There was just the little matter of persuading Dawn to leave Triple Creek until he returned. Dawn had already told him in no uncertain terms that nothing would drive her away from the ranch, yet for her own safety he had to change her mind. His previous experience of his stepsister's stubbornness left him with no illusions of how difficult a task that would be.

4

THE stranger, dressed in black, rode slowly and carefully up to the ranch. Only after he was fairly sure that the ranch was deserted did he dismount. Even then it was a considerable distance from the ranch house. As he walked towards the house, he began to whistle a Dixie marching tune. He was very careful to ensure that if there were people in the house then they could clearly see that his hand was well away from his Remington six-gun. The stranger had already found out about Triple Creek's part in the range war and its stand against the Yankee-owned Lazy K. He whistled louder in the hope that a Southern sympathizer was less likely to be mistaken for a new gunhand of the Lazy K, and therefore, less likely to be shot at.

Many times during the Civil War,

the stranger had approached ranches in similar fashion, usually to lure the occupants into a false sense of security while he found out whether the place was worth raiding. Or so his enemies claimed and he had many of those. Indeed, it seemed that all hands were turned against those who had ridden for Quantrill. There was no denying Quantrill's savagery, yet hadn't others done things almost as bad? What had he done that was so much worse than General Sheridan's men when they laid waste to the Shenandoah Valley? Plantations burnt to the ground and their Negroes driven off, whether they wanted to go or not. Today, Sheridan's actions were well respected, while he was a reviled and much wanted outlaw. To the stranger, the only real difference was that Sheridan and his men were on the winning side.

To his surprise he found Triple Creek deserted, just as the Running Dog ranch had been when he visited it earlier. The stranger searched the ranch thoroughly.

Yet he took nothing, not even any of the ammunition that Rowdy had stashed away in the ruined barn. He was pleasantly surprised when he found the unusual .42 calibre bullets for they matched one of his own weapons. This unusual calibre had been almost exclusively used by the Confederacy, confirming that the sympathy of its owner lay with the South. He returned the ammunition to its hiding-place; for once stealing was not his purpose. So he left the Triple Creek ranch exactly as he had found it. He was well content with his morning's work but would what he had found be of any use to his brother? Would his brother want to use either ranch as a hideout? He would soon know for he had arranged to meet him in a little over an hour. He left, riding at a hard gallop. Though they were very close, his brother was not a man to be kept waiting.

The dust had hardly settled as Dawn and Rowdy returned. They were completely unaware of the stranger's visit as they unsaddled the horses and entered the kitchen. Rowdy was tired. At Dawn's suggestion he rested in his father's room. Overcome by fatigue, he fell asleep at once. Dawn awoke him with the news that dinner was ready. It was the third meal running that had been cooked for him. A pleasant change from eating alone on the trail.

During dinner Dawn was particularly quiet. Rowdy noted that she had changed again and she was now wearing a simple white dress. She had combed out her long red hair so now it almost reached the middle of her back. Dinner consisted of roast chicken and boiled potatoes washed down with a glass of root beer. While he was eating he put off the subject of Dawn moving to the safety of the Indian Mountains. When he finally plucked up courage she instantly flew into a fearful rage, just as he had feared she would.

"No! No! No! I won't leave Triple Creek. Besides, how do I know if I can trust you, ranch boy? How do I know that you won't leave again and not come back for years, like last time? Then the Lazy K would walk in and take over. No, I stay here and that's all there is to it. You've not been back a day and already you're telling me what to do. I won't move, and that's final!"

"OK! I know when I'm beaten." Rowdy raised his arms in mock surrender in an attempt to defuse her anger.

"What! Don't tell me you're going to give in without a fight, ranch boy?" Dawn's face was a picture of disbelief.

"Yes, I give in, but if you keep calling me ranch boy, you might find yourself across my knees," said Rowdy, but he was smiling.

"It would take more than you to do that; besides I might like it," she said, grinning cheekily.

Even so she was careful not to call him ranch boy again that evening. In fact it was to be many years before she used that name again. When she did, it would not be in anger.

"Dawn, what's happened to the Running Dog ranch?"

Rowdy asked the question as casually as he could. Not that it did him any good, she saw through his next move almost before he had started it.

"No, I'm not going to the Running Dog ranch either," snapped Dawn. "In any case there's been some odd goings on over there. Just a few days ago I saw a stranger riding across Bottom Creek and on to their range."

"So what's odd about that?" asked Rowdy.

"Well, Bottom Creek has been dried up since last summer so there's no Running Dog cattle down there. Not that he looked like a cowboy," said Dawn.

"Drifter or perhaps gunman?" he asked.

"Definitely not a drifter. He was dressed completely in black, more like a top gunman."

"It's a puzzle, but then so is Bottom

Creek drying up. There used to be a group of springs feeding it from Hawks Ridge," said Rowdy.

"Never heard of that place," replied Dawn.

"Just my name for it. I found it in the Indian Mountains when I was a boy. I'll take you there one day, when all the troubles with the Lazy K are over. It's hard to get there but well worth the effort," said Rowdy.

"I'll look forward to that," said Dawn.

Whether Dawn meant she was looking forward to the trip or the end of the troubles with the Lazy K, Rowdy couldn't tell. For some reason he didn't ask, perhaps because he had not sorted out his feelings towards his stepsister. He no longer disliked her, quite the opposite, yet there were times when he felt uneasy in her company.

Rowdy let the moment slip by, much to Dawn's disappointment. She was about to try another tack when she realized that her stepbrother was worried about something. It was clear to her that there was something on his mind so this was not the time to start flirting or teasing. Again she felt disappointed though she had no idea why.

Rowdy's cavalry-trained mind was full of undigested information. He tried to work out a strategy to keep Dawn and Triple Creek safe while he returned to Richmond. Unfortunately, Dawn kept breaking his concentration. Unlike most women he had known, her conversation was stimulating and demanding his attention. As a result he could not focus on the problems ahead. Going back into Clearwater would be no better, for Anne Lattimer had demonstrated a different form of stimulation to keep him occupied.

Then it hit him like a flash of lightning. He had the solution. If Dawn would not go to the Indian Mountains, or to the safety of the town, then the town must come to her. However, it would have to be in a way that would not seem to challenge the Lazy K. He had the answer to that too; his idea should ensure that the Lazy K would not come back to trouble the Triple Creek ranch for a little while at least. As there was nothing to be done until morning he relaxed and spent the evening talking about the old days with his stepsister. It felt good to be a part of a family again.

A blanket of white mist hung over the ranch next morning but by the time he had hitched the old horse to the storekeeper's rig it had begun to clear. Awkwardly he took his leave of Dawn. He did not tell her about his plans, fearing her objections would delay him even further. He wanted to take her in his arms, hug her and tell her that he would be back to stay. However, he couldn't for it wouldn't be true. His return from Richmond could only be temporary, duty would call him away again. After the war he had chosen to become a Texas Ranger, summarily dispensing law and order where otherwise there was none. Only recently he accepted a commission in the new US Cavalry; there his role to maintain law and order would be much the same.

He had been travelling for barely thirty minutes, when from out from of a distant thicket of trees, rode a stranger dressed in black. Rowdy assumed it was the stranger Dawn had seen riding along Bottom Creek. He was not aware that this was the man who had watched his run-in with the two gunmen in Clearwater.

Something about him made Rowdy regret that he had left his rifle and carbine with the Lattimers. True he had the shotgun, but lethal as it was at close quarters, it was useless at long range. The stranger was not about to let him get close enough to use it and held up his hand, ordering Rowdy to stop. The other hand of the stranger hovered inches away from the butt of his Remington. At that range it was more a gesture than a threat.

"Pardon the interruption, friend," shouted the stranger, still at least 300 yards away, "but we would appreciate a little of your time. Would you care for some good Southern-style coffee in exchange for a little information?"

Only in the trashy dime stories written about Rowdy had he drawn his six-gun and killed a man at 300 yards. That was rubbish, just for the readers back East. In real life his .36 calibre Whitney didn't have accuracy or the range to hit a man at anything like that distance. Then there was the 'we' heavily stressed by the black-clothed rider. No doubt there was at least one other man hidden in the thicket with a rifle trained on him. That man would be waiting for Rowdy to make the slightest wrong move. There was no other choice: he had to agree to the stranger's request. For once Rowdy was glad that he was wearing his tattered clothes. Perhaps he would be mistaken for an ordinary drifter.

"Sure friend," drawled Rowdy

adopting the Texas drawl he used when posing as a drifter. "I would sure appreciate you keeping your gun hand where I can see it. Wouldn't want there to be any unfortunate misunderstandings."

Rowdy drove the wagon towards the thicket and dismounted. He left the horse untethered by a clump of fresh grass. Remembering how it had stopped to graze in the middle of the confrontation with the Lazy K gunmen, he was sure it would not stray. Besides he might not have time to unhitch the horse if things went wrong.

The gunman led him into a ravine at the back of the thicket. At the bottom of the ravine was a camp-fire. A second gunman sat beside it. He offered Rowdy a mug of scalding hot coffee without saying a word. He didn't have to, because they had met before. Like his brother, the second gunman had ridden for Quantrill and had met Rowdy, then a captain, during the war. So there was little point in Rowdy still pretending he was a drifter. The second gunman knew that he was the famous Rowdy Carter.

The first gunman sat down near to Rowdy but on the opposite side to his brother, thus making it impossible for Rowdy to draw on them at the same time. Clearly they were professionals and were taking no chances. There was nothing that Rowdy could do, so he relaxed and sipped hot coffee.

"How can I help you?" asked Rowdy, reverting to his normal accent.

"That's mighty nice of you friend," said the first gunman. "We need information, but the folks round here ain't partial to strangers asking questions, especially if they're from the South."

"Wasn't always like that, only since this Major Norton took over the Lazy K," said Rowdy.

"So tell us," said the stranger.

Rowdy told the two most of what he knew about the changes that had happened in Clearwater. He explained that he had been away for some years and was just visiting his father's ranch. Since he had previously met the second man during the war there was no point in denying that he was Rowdy Carter. The gunmen seemed satisfied with his story and offered him a second mug of coffee. They only asked one further question.

"What happened to the family that used to run the store?" asked the second gunman speaking for the first time. The coldness of his voice sent an icy chill tingling down the Rowdy's spine.

"Murdered. The new storekeeper hinted that it was because they were Southern sympathizers. It's a great shame. I liked the James family, they were good friends to me when I was a boy."

"You've helped a lot. Now is there anything you want to know about us?" asked the other gunman.

"Not a thing, friend; I figure that too much of the wrong type of information can be dangerous to your health," said

Rowdy laughing.

"Fair enough, friend. You can leave anytime you want," said the second gunman.

Rowdy needed no second bidding and was soon on his way. He was under no illusion as to the true nature of his recent companions. Although there were only two of them he knew that they posed a far more dangerous threat than any of the Lazy K gunmen. If possible he must do nothing to antagonize them should they meet again. Rowdy had an idea who they were. If his guess was correct he had been in more danger during the last few minutes than at any time since the end of the Civil War.

The delay caused by the two meant that Rowdy had lost much precious time. Even so, he slowed the storekeeper's wagon as soon as he was sure that the two gunmen were not following him. There was no point in killing the old horse. The time lost could not be made up, so he would have to delay his departure. The Lattimers were the key to Rowdy's plan and he would need time to persuade them.

It was mid afternoon when Rowdy drove the wagon into a deserted Clearwater. He returned the wagon to the storekeeper and walked to the Lattimers' house. The smell of dinner cooking reminded him that he had not eaten since breakfast. Luckily he was invited to eat as soon as he entered the house.

Over dinner Rowdy outlined his plan, leaving out the key role the former sheriff of Clearwater was expected to play. Bill Lattimer considered it thoughtfully, although Anne seemed less than impressed. She wore a prim and unflattering gingham dress, her long black hair tied tightly back behind her ears. She looked like a typical schoolteacher so often portrayed in the dime novels back East. Rowdy noticed that her attitude towards him had cooled considerably since the other night. Today, she was more like the Anne of old, polite and aloof. Perhaps he had upset her by restraining his natural desires and not returning her passion in full. Dawn and Anne had both troubled him greatly when a boy, now that he was a grown man nothing had changed. He still did not understand either of them!

"It seems a sound enough plan," said Bill Lattimer interrupting Rowdy's train of thought, "but there's one serious flaw in it."

"What's that?" asked Rowdy innocently.

"It's going to take a few days to recruit the right men and get them started at Triple Creek. In any case you couldn't leave them there unsupervised while you rode to Richmond."

"That's where you come in," said Rowdy, smiling because Bill had taken the bait.

"Sorry, you've lost me, Rod," replied the former sheriff. He still used Rowdy's childhood name.

"He wants you to do it, don't you,

Rod?" said Anne. She smiled at Rowdy for the first time since his return.

"Of course," said Rowdy. "You know the best men to choose, four should be enough."

"And who could be better to supervise them and keep an eye on Dawn?" said Anne.

"Exactly," said Rowdy.

"But what could I do if there was trouble with the Lazy K?" asked Bill. There was bitterness in his voice as he held up his half-empty sleeve.

The smile on Anne's face changed to a look of deep concern. She need not have worried for Rowdy had foreseen this line of argument and was prepared accordingly. During the war he had been called upon to produce campaign plans for Mosby. He had quickly learnt to anticipate all the possible campaign problems and how to overcome them. On the occasions he had failed to do so, he had felt the cutting edge of the general's wrath. It had been a good training ground and now he deftly brushed aside Bill's objection.

"I don't anticipate that there will be too much trouble. After all, you will be repairing the property which Major Norton aims to take over. If you don't, someone at the Lazy K will have to," said Rowdy.

"You could be right, young Rod. I've not met a gunman who is that fond of hard work," said the former sheriff.

"If the Lazy K comes too close you can use this," said Rowdy handing over his shotgun. "There's plenty of ammunition at the ranch."

"So there's nothing more to say, is there?" said Anne quickly, to forestall any further objections her father might raise. "Father, why not start now while the town is quiet? You might get the recruiting done before anyone on the Lazy K finds out."

"Well, I would like to give Tom Handy and his boy a chance to work. They live out of town at the staging-post. They're good workers, or would be, if people would employ them.

But after what happened to the James couple everyone is scared to employ anyone from the South. Tom Handy needs money to open up the stage depot again and I'd trust both of them with my life," said the former sheriff.

"Talking of money, I'd better give you enough to get the job done," said Rowdy.

He went to the outhouse and retrieved his saddle-bags. One of them still bulged with money but he had made quite a hole in the loot he had acquired during the war. By the time he returned, Bill Lattimer was ready to go. Anne busied herself clearing up the dishes. Rowdy gave the former sheriff sufficient money to hire men and buy materials. Bill left immediately and walked to the store to hire its rig. He intended to load it with the goods he required for Triple Creek before setting out for the staging-post. The former sheriff hoped that a wagonful of materials would convince the Handys that Triple Creek was back in business.

Anne watched her father walk purposefully to the front gate. He turned and smiled at her. To Anne it seemed that a heavy weight had fallen off her father's shoulders. In putting her father in charge of Triple Creek, Rowdy had made her father feel worthwhile again. She felt very grateful to the man who had drifted back into their lives. There would be ample time to show that gratitude since it was clear to Anne that her father would not be back for several hours. Anne returned to the living-room. She had a plan of her own.

"I'm just going to change, Rod; there's warm water in the kitchen if you want to clean up," she said.

He did just that though his tattered reb clothes were beyond repair. His ploy wearing the ragged dress of a Confederate soldiers had only worked up to a point. He had hoped to go about his business in Clearwater unnoticed, just another drifter. Events had overtaken him and this ploy had failed. Yet the ragged reb clothes had served him well during his meeting with the Southern gunmen. Even so, he would be glad to discard them once and for all when he returned to Richmond.

When Anne returned she had changed into a simple white shirt and black skirt. Her long black hair hung loosely down her back but it was the totally unbuttoned shirtfront that grabbed Rowdy's attention.

"There's a lot that you don't know about me, Rowdy Carter. I'd rather you found out at first hand what I'm really like than from some gossip-mongering busybody," she said.

Rowdy was stunned by Anne's unexpected forwardness. Apart from his stepmother, there had only been three types of women in his life: saloon girls who would do almost anything for money, society women who would do anything for a thrill, providing it was done discreetly, and finally respectable women who did not go around with shirts undone. But Anne, the supposedly respectable schoolteacher, had only just begun. She smiled as he gazed at her unbuttoned shirt, then slowly undid her skirt and stepped out of it as it slid to the floor. She posed provocatively ensuring that he could see the perfection of her almost naked body.

"Rowdy, it will be hours before Father returns, so why don't you take me to bed? I want to show you what you've been missing all these years."

He did just that. Naked, Anne was a beautiful and sexy woman. In bed she was wild, adventurous and spontaneous in everything she did. Yet amid all the passion, good though that was, there was something missing. Had he not always wanted Anne? Now she was in bed with him, willing to make love, again and again. So what was wrong? During the long ride to Richmond he asked himself that question time after time. Never once did he find the answer.

5

ALTHOUGH Rowdy took only the necessities with him on the long journey, it was still a heavy load for any horse to carry. The Henry rifle and the Spencer carbine were in the slings behind Rowdy. Two full waterbottles were slung on the saddle in front of him. One of his saddle-holsters carried his Le Mat, the other held gold coins and extra ammunition instead of his old Colt. In its place he carried the Whitney. It was attached to a Mexican style gun-belt, which hung from his left shoulder down across his chest to his right hip. Experience had taught him that the Mexican rig enabled him to reload much quicker while on horseback. However, on foot, the weight of the rig was often a severe handicap.

It was a heavy load for Black Bart to

carry, yet the huge stallion made light of it. The great beast's mood was as ugly as his looks. Once again, they had left Black Bart's lifelong friend, the pack-mule, behind. Speed was of the essence so Rowdy skirted all the settlements on the way to Richmond. By avoiding people he hoped to eliminate any delays on the way. During the journey he lived off the land, shooting an occasional turkey or wild fowl.

So it was a leaner and scruffier than ever Rowdy who entered Richmond late one night. He went directly to his old quarters, and stabled his horse. He was acutely conscious of his filthy and ragged appearance so he remained in the stable for the rest of the night, bedding down on the hay in the loft. Below him, Black Bart began to munch hay. Perverse as ever, the great horse preferred it to grass. Although it had been a long, hard ride, the huge beast had taken it in his stride and was fresher than his rider in every way.

Early next morning Rowdy was

awakened by the sound of activity below. It was the stable boy coming to groom the horses before they were taken out for their morning exercise. Unlike most horses Black Bart hated being groomed and snorted his displeasure as the young stable boy desperately tried to calm him. The black stallion reared high above the boy, but the young lad stood his ground without flinching. Seeing that the boy was not going to be frightened off, Black Bart kicked out his right hind leg in annoyance, sending a grooming stool clattering into the stable wall.

"Enough of that, you beast from hell," snapped Rowdy from the hayloft.

Immediately the great beast lowered its head and began to eat what was left of the hay. Although it was still an important military post, in some respects discipline was slack. Horses were frequently left overnight for grooming the next day. It was a privilege accorded to senior officers. So a strange horse was not unusual and had drawn no comment from the stable boy. However, the same could not be said for Rowdy's dishevelled appearance as he climbed down from the hayloft.

"Sorry, Mister, senior officers' horses only," said the stable boy. "You must leave at once or I'll have to report you to the sergeant. You're not supposed to be in here."

"That's all right, lad," said a deep booming voice from the open stable door.

It was a huge, black, master sergeant, very smartly dressed in the new uniform of the United States Cavalry. He had heard the commotion kicked up by Black Bart and had come to investigate. The sergeant recognized the great beast instantly and walked over to him, patting him gently. Black Bart would have dealt savagely with anyone else taking such a liberty but he knew better than to tangle with the massive Sergeant Ellis Browne. He had done so once before when he was a colt and he had felt the wrath of the sergeant. Apart from his master, whom he tolerated with much bad grace, the massive sergeant was the only man Black Bart respected and obeyed.

"Now, sir, this won't do, won't do at all," said Sergeant Browne.

He spoke in a cultured and well-educated manner, very unusual for a Negro born in the South. But then Ellis Browne was a one off. Born on a Virginian plantation, his parents had been treated like family rather than slaves. On the plantation, young Ellis had received the same private tutoring as his master's children. When Mosby, then a colonel, formed the Irregulars, Ellis Browne opted to join them rather than fight for the North. However, during the Civil War he rarely carried a gun. In the South there were many who despised slavery, but armed Negroes were unacceptable to all but the most liberal-minded Southerner. When Rowdy had been appointed Captain in the Irregulars, he made Ellis Browne his sergeant, a position in which he had excelled, even though rank signified less than ability in the South's only undefeated army.

"Good to see you again, Sergeant."

"We've been expecting you, sir. Can't blame the boy for not recognizing you as an officer. Beg pardon, sir, but you look like something the cat dragged in. Perhaps you'd like to slip along to the sergeants' quarters right away? I'll have a bath run for you and have your new major's uniform laid out."

It was hardly a request. Sergeant Ellis Browne looked after his officers as if they were his own children. Without appearing to be disrespectful, that's how he treated them, like children. Woe betide an officer whose conduct or appearance demeaned the United States Cavalry. Nor would he tolerate abuse of the enlisted men by any officer. Though only a sergeant, discipline at the headquarters was left entirely in his hands. A hard but just taskmaster, Ellis Browne was highly respected, although not without enemies.

The sergeant had once been charged with insubordination. Although a Northerner, one newly promoted officer, a Major Norton, found it difficult to accept that a coloured man should have risen to the rank of sergeant and thus be in a position to give orders to a white man. The major took the first chance he had to reduce Browne to the ranks but the punishment was short lived.

Major Norton was soon summoned to the presence of his commanding officer who then proceeded to read out an urgent dispatch. This dispatch ordered the major to reinstate Ellis Browne or resign. It finished by stating that the sergeant was more use to the cavalry than the major. The dispatch was signed by General Ulysses S. Grant. No one ever discovered any link between the general and Sergeant Browne nor how the general had found out about his demotion. However, after that, no one ever questioned Ellis Browne's right to instruct officers on their conduct.

Soon after his rebuttal, Major Norton resigned. A few weeks later it was discovered that a shipment of arms together with a significant sum of money entrusted to Major Norton had gone missing. Nothing was ever proved against the major, who had in any case departed the scene. Yet soon afterwards Norton was able to purchase the Lazy K. Even at its give-away price, the vast Lazy K ranch should have been far above the reach of anyone who lived solely on the pay of a major.

As instructed, Rowdy made his way to the sergeants' quarters. A hot bath was made ready for him. While he was in the tub, an orderly discreetly removed his old clothes. The orderly returned a few minutes later with a new uniform, boots and sabre. Rowdy dried himself and put on the new uniform.

He was no longer the ill-clad drifter, he was Major Carter. He knew that whatever the future held he would never again become the drifter. That part of his past was gone forever. However, the legend of Rowdy Carter would be less easier to live down. The fame he had enjoyed in the past plus his new obligations in the cavalry meant that it would be a long time, if ever, before he could settle down. The question was, did he want to and if so, with whom?

The uniform fitted perfectly though the sabre felt awkward. Rowdy felt the sabre served little useful purpose. In common with many in the Confederacy he had discarded it for a double-barrelled shotgun. Yet the sabre had been favoured by the Union and was now standard issue in the new United States Cavalry.

Sergeant Browne entered carrying a grey, plumed hat. It was far removed from the standard issue peaked blue, boxed hat. Seeing Rowdy smartly dressed in his new uniform and wearing the sabre, the sergeant's face broke into an approving smile.

"That's much better, Major Carter, sir. Now we look like the officer and gentleman that we are, don't we sir?"

"Don't sound so smug, Ellis, you know wearing the blue goes against the grain. As for this damn thing, it should be dumped in the nearest river," Rowdy pointed to his sabre.

"Beg pardon, sir. Standing orders state that ceremonial tunic and sabre shall be worn at all times when in headquarters. There is no such order relating to headwear, so I thought that you might prefer this one. It's the same style that General Mosby used to wear, sir."

"Yes, I remember. It will do fine, Ellis. By the way what's all this *sir* business? It used to be plain Rowdy."

"You're a major now, sir, and this is not the Irregulars. Wouldn't be good for discipline if the men heard me call you by your Confederate nickname, now would it, sir?" said the sergeant.

"I suppose you're right, Sergeant, but we did pretty well in the Irregulars without fancy titles, didn't we? So when there are no enlisted men, or officers senior to myself present, call me Rowdy again. That's an order, Sergeant."

Rowdy was not about to win. Sergeant Browne was a past master at seeming to agree to an order, yet still getting his own way.

"Certainly, sir. Now would the major like breakfast? I've arranged for one to be made for you in the sergeants' mess."

Master Sergeant Ellis Browne led the way to the mess and went in closing the door behind him. Rowdy, resplendent in his brand new uniform, stopped at the door. He knocked loudly on it. In doing so he was observing a tradition as old as the cavalry.

"Officer at the door. Permission to enter," he called.

Sergeant Browne opened the door

and invited him in.

"Officer, present," the sergeant called.

As Major Rowdy Carter entered the mess all the other sergeants stood to attention. Again tradition demanded that they should do so. Rowdy gave the traditional response.

"At ease, gentlemen, as you were. While I'm a guest in your mess, be pleased to carry on as normal."

The formalities over, the sergeants' mess returned to normal. It was not merely a trivial ritual that Rowdy had observed. It re-enforced the role of the senior non-commissioned officers, without whom no army could function properly. It was a privilege the NCOs guarded jealousy. Any officer failing to observe it soon found out his mistake. Suddenly life became much harder as the NCOs followed his every order to the exact letter, but did nothing else. Soon the officer was having to issue orders for every single routine action or nothing happened at all. By common consent, none of the other officers intervened, making life intolerable for the unfortunate man.

An apology was not deemed appropriate for breaking what was only an unofficial custom. So, to redeem himself, the hapless officer was obliged to return to the sergeants' mess. After making sure that he was invited inside, he was then obliged to buy drinks for all the senior NCOs during the rest of the evening. Major Norton had been one officer who had broken the code and suffered accordingly.

After breakfast, Rowdy reported to the commanding officer, Colonel Bradley, and presented him with his leave of absence. Colonel Bradley was a seasoned veteran who had first seen active service in the Texas-Mexico war. He listened intently to the major's story and immediately agreed to Rowdy taking three months' leave before taking up his new command at Fort Smith. However, as Rowdy expected, the colonel could offer little else in the way of practical assistance.

"We are seriously short of experienced troopers as it is, Major, so I cannot offer you any men for the moment, but leave it with me for a few days and I'll see if anything can be arranged."

Two days turned into three, then four, but still no word came from the colonel. Not that Rowdy was left alone to his own devices. Far from it, his fellow officers reintroduced him into the society life of Richmond. Maybe it was not quite as glittering as during the time he had served with General Stuart, but the great society evenings made it seem as if the Civil War had never happened. Yet Rowdy no longer enjoyed the entertainment as much as he had once done. Nevertheless, his life became a whirl of social engagements. He was surprised to find that he was still a celebrity and much in demand by the society ladies of Richmond. They invited him to their social functions by evening and their beds by night. Rowdy refused all offers of that sort. Attractive as many of his hostesses were, he was no longer interested in them.

After several days Colonel Bradley sent for Rowdy. However, when Rowdy entered the colonel's office and saluted, the colonel remained seated and barely responded, he seemed displeased.

"Major, I understand that you are trying to hire gunmen. Thinking of starting your own war?"

"No, sir."

"Glad to hear it. Can't have civilians getting in the way of our troops, so we will have no more of hiring nonsense and that's an order."

The colonel went on to outline his plan which involved sending new recruits to Clearwater as soon as Sergeant Ellis had completed their training. As this was still a few weeks away Rowdy would be allowed to return home at once.

Colonel Bradley had been obliged to obtain permission from Washington for his plan. Unfortunately, Major Norton had well placed informants there. They soon learnt of the plan. Worse still, the delay in sending the troops to Clearwater gave the major ample time to prepare a special welcoming party for them.

6

AS Major Norton had promised, the buyer had paid a good price for the herd. Jack Denton paid off his drovers, keeping only his top hand and his two longest serving cowboys. They would be needed to tend the stock left behind to produce the next herd. There was plenty of money in his saddle-bags to pay off the Running Dog mortgage. Even after that, Jack was certain that there would be enough left to ensure the survival of the Running Dog ranch for at least two years when there should be another herd to sell.

Major Norton and his gunmen remained in Dodge City to celebrate. The major had no financial problems to worry about and, unlike Jack Denton, had left sufficient men behind to take care of any problems on the Lazy K in his absence. Of course the major was completely unaware of the return of Rowdy Carter, otherwise he might have changed his plans.

A few days' hard riding brought Jack Denton's party to the edge of the Wastelands. Unwisely, they decided to save time. Instead of taking the longer but safer route down the Arkansas river to Fort Smith, they headed across the Wastelands. Just before nightfall they met John Carter. Though he was still weak, he had ridden across the Wastelands to warn Jack that the Lazy K had attempted to obtain Triple Creek's water-rights and their attack on him.

Unfortunately, the warning came too late. John Carter had been spotted leaving the Indian Mountains by one of the many outlaws in the pay of Major Norton. The information was passed by relay to Rex Morden who was already in the Wastelands hiring more outlaws for the major. Morden and his newly hired gang tracked John

Carter, so Jack Denton learnt of the major's real plans, learnt the hard way when their camp was raided that night. Why the gunmen wore masks was a mystery, because they left nobody alive to tell the story of their raid. After the raid, one of the gunmen picked up the saddle-bags containing the money from the sale of the Running Dog herd. Only when they were well clear of the massacre did he remove his mask. It was Rex Morden.

After the massacre, Morden and one of the outlaws headed rapidly towards Dodge. He knew that Major Norton would be delighted to get his hands on the money. The others, led by a renegade called Warlock Sims, returned at a more leisurely pace towards Clearwater. There was much work for them to do, in and around Clearwater, not honest decent work, but the sort of pillaging that even Major Norton and his gunmen would not do. However, the major was willing to pay Sims and his gang very well to do it.

Backshooting and pillage were second nature to Sims. Rape and something even worse were his favourite pastimes. Being hired to do it by Major Norton's top gunhand was merely a bonus. Sims had already planned to raid Clearwater. Of course, he kept that information from Rex Morden. When the time was right Warlock Sims intended to deal with Morden and anyone else who got in his way. The thought of the mayhem he was going to wreak on Clearwater made his lips drool with pleasure. He could hardly wait to get started. Certainly not long enough to bury the bodies of the men he had helped kill.

★ ★ ★

It was the buzzards circling high overhead that first attracted Kital to the camp-site. He had followed John Carter over the Indian Mountains and across the Wastelands. Even though he was no longer a young man and was on foot, Kital had been less than a day behind the only white man he called friend. He saw the tracks left by the outlaws' horses and followed them towards the circling buzzards.

Kital found only death and destruction at the camp-site. Amongst the dead bodies lay John Denton, killed instantly by a bullet in his back. Neither he, nor any of the other dead men had drawn their guns, such had been the speed of the attack by the outlaws.

Without a shovel the ground was too hard to dig graves. So Kital covered the bodies with rocks. He made two separate piles. Under the smaller pile lay the body of John Carter; Jack Denton and his cowhands lay under the larger pile. It was hard work, but as soon as he had finished, Kital began the ritual death dance of the Running Dog Indians. It was the highest tribute he could pay John Carter and the only time the old medicine man performed the ritual for a white man. The death dance lasted for hours, but Kital never once paused. Only when it was finally over did he sink to the ground. Completely exhausted, he fell into a deep sleep.

It was dawn when he awoke. Without a glance at the graves Kital began the long journey back to Triple Creek. Breaking the tragic news to Dawn would not be a pleasant task. Until he had done so, he would neither eat nor sleep. Not once did he look back at the graves, nor would he ever return to visit them. In his eyes, the spirit of John Carter was now in the hunting lodges of his forefathers. Soon he would celebrate that event in the Indian Mountains, in the sacred meeting place of the Running Dog Indians.

7

MOONLIGHT filtered through the clouds temporarily bathing Hawks Ridge in silver light. A lone rider clad in buckskin, rode cautiously into the trees at the top of the Ridge. The rider gazed across the valley, looking for guards. He saw nothing except the dam. As Rowdy had guessed, a large wooden dam had been constructed to contain the natural spring water that had once run down the valley to form Bottom Creek.

Bottom Creek was once the largest of the three creeks from which the Triple Creek ranch derived its name. It ran across the northern ranges of the ranch and carried on until it fed into Squaw Lake, on the Running Dog ranch. During each spring, water formed by the winter snows of the Indian Mountains flooded through Bottom Creek turning it into a raging torrent. Now that torrent was trapped behind a dam which had a sophisticated sluice system. This let the extra flood water into a canal which flowed into another valley. This valley had also been blocked by an even larger dam, so new, it was barely less than half full. It was evident that the second dam would absorb virtually all the spring flood waters from the first dam for several years. Of course, the second dam would eventually fill up, but by that time, the Running Dog ranch would have been ruined.

Only two parties stood to gain when the Running Dog ranch became bankrupt: the bank who held its mortgage and Major Norton. The owner of the Lazy K would be able to buy the Running Dog ranch from the bank at a fraction of its real price, yet the bank would still make a handsome profit. After he had purchased the Running Dog ranch, all the major had to do was to wait for the second dam to fill. Once that had happened, the water would automatically flow back into Bottom Creek. Then the flood waters of the following spring would refill Squaw Lake and the Running Dog would become a viable ranch again.

The only minor flaw in the major's plan was that the water first had to flow across Triple Creek before it reached the Running Dog ranch. The major must have realized that it was possible for Triple Creek to divert the course of Bottom Creek to prevent that from happening, hence his desire to obtain the water-rights of the ranch.

The second dam had taken Rowdy by surprise. He had come prepared to blow up one dam but fortunately he had sufficient dynamite strapped to his back to blow both. Even so the second meant that he had to change his plan. In any case there was far too much water in the first dam to blow it up. He dared not risk sending thousands of tons of water cascading down the steep valley as it would do untold damage, killing anyone and anything in its path. No, there had to be another way.

As the clouds again obscured the moon, Rowdy moved silently to the sluice gate. There was no sign of guards but experience had taught him always to be cautious. Rather than placing all the dynamite at the bottom of the dam as he had originally planned, he lodged three sticks in an outcrop of rock situated high above the sluice gate. Instead of setting a fuse, he left the dynamite where it could be easily seen when daylight came.

Rowdy scrambled up the face of Hawks Ridge for about a hundred feet until he came to a massive rock face. There, directly above the canal that diverted the water to the second dam, he placed the bulk of the dynamite. Again he left the dynamite plainly visible. Carefully, he returned through the trees to where he had left Black Bart. The great horse had easily completed the return trip from Richmond but was less than pleased when Rowdy had ridden into the Indian Mountains. The great stallion was prairie bred so regarded mountains as only suitable for goats.

Black Bart snorted disgustedly, then pawed the ground to show his displeasure as his master rode even higher into the mountains. It was a trail that Rowdy had often used during his childhood yet he still found it difficult to pick his way through the shadows cast by the fir trees. The antics of Black Bart did not help.

Rowdy's nerves were stretched to their limit. Were there any guards he had missed? His earlier run in with the Lazy K gunmen seemed not to have made any lasting impression. Perhaps he had been wrong and Barnabus Reno had not yet told the major about their business deal. If so, Rowdy's ragged clothes might just have fooled the Lazy K gunhands into thinking he was just another drifter who had moved on. Anyway, the dam seemed to be unguarded.

It was dawn by the time the trail led Rowdy to the opposite side of Hawks Ridge. He dismounted and, taking aim with his Henry rifle, fired at the dynamite in the rocks above the sluice gate. Rowdy was a crack shot and the Henry rifle had been the best repeating rifle of the Civil War. Yet Rowdy missed it, the bullet hitting the hillside several feet to the right. Though it was barely 300 yards to the other side of the valley, Rowdy missed again. Much to his disgust, he had over corrected and the bullet thudded into the rock again missing the dynamite. It was just as well Ellis Browne was not watching, or the sergeant would have sent him with the rookies to practise on the rifle range.

The third shot hit the dynamite. It exploded violently, sending huge rocks hurtling into the air. Most of them fell on to the sluice gate smashing it to smithereens, before crashing into the dam and creating great plumes of water. The water trapped behind the sluice gate shot into the air forming a waterfall which fell directly into the canal that led to the second dam.

It was several minutes before the force of the water began to decrease. When it had slowed sufficiently to be safe, Rowdy took aim and fired at the second pile of dynamite above the canal. Although it was much further away, Rowdy's first shot was true. The explosion was deafening, sending clouds of dust and smoke into the air. Unlike the previous explosion, the dynamite caused a massive landslide and it seemed as if half the mountain had fallen into the canal. As the dust began to settle, Rowdy smiled with satisfaction. The canal had been buried under thousands of tons of rock. The dam water cascaded out of the shattered sluice and poured into the original river bed. A mass of white foam, it roared down the valley, through Bottom Creek and then sped on to Squaw Lake.

The sluice gate was shattered beyond repair. It would take a large band of workers several weeks, if not months, to dig through the rubble now blocking the canal — always supposing the work was allowed to proceed without interruption and Rowdy was determined that would not be the case.

If he could prevent the clearance of the rubble and the repair of the sluice gate until winter, snowfalls would then cause all work to stop until next spring. By then it would be too late, for as the thaw came, the spring waters would flood through the shattered sluice gate and down into Bottom Creek. That ought to provide sufficient water for the next Running Dog herd during the dry summer months.

Rowdy spent the rest of the morning watching the effects of his handiwork. Much to his surprise no one came from the Lazy K. So at noon, well satisfied with the results of his work, he headed for Triple Creek.

He hardly recognized the ranch; there were signs of improvement everywhere. The corral fences had been mended and painted white, as had both the main house and the bunkhouse. The little garden had been weeded and replanted. Only the barn remained as it was, yet even there he could see piles of timber stacked high in preparation for the rebuilding of that derelict structure.

Rowdy slowly approached his old home. He rode in cautiously, not wishing to alarm the occupants. This time he needn't have worried. As he neared the house, Anne Lattimer appeared at the main door and let out a whoop of joy as she recognized him. Behind her appeared two men he did not recognize. Following them was Anne's father with Rowdy's shotgun held in his one good hand. Rowdy was disappointed that there was no sign of Dawn.

Anne's welcome was as unrestrained as their first reunion. She raced to meet Rowdy, flinging her arms around him as soon as he dismounted. Black Bart snorted in disgust at the display of emotion. The massive black horse still had not forgiven his master for not following the cute filly they had met during their first day back in Clearwater. Even so, Black Bart was glad to be back and reunited with his lifelong companion, the pack-mule.

Rowdy was shown to his old room, now normally occupied by Dawn. However, most of her things had gone. Puzzled and disappointed by her absence, Rowdy washed, shaved and took a bath using the water in the bathtub someone had already filled. He would have preferred to use the shower next to the bunkhouse, but that would have seemed ungrateful.

After his bath he found that someone had brought him a complete set of new clothes which he was only too glad to put on. He had been wearing the same buckskins ever since he had left Richmond and they reeked. His new military uniform was still packed in his saddle-bags. However, he did not want to advertise his appointment as major. Not only did it seem too much like showing off, it would also be an indication that, all too soon, he would have to leave.

After a short rest he went for the evening meal. The smell of steak reminded him that he had been living rough and hadn't eaten a proper meal since he had left Richmond. He was getting soft. There was still no sign of Dawn or his father as Rowdy entered the main room. The table had been set for four. Tom and Clem Handy ate in the bunkhouse, his father and Dawn were not on the ranch, so for whom was the other place set?

Bill Lattimer sat down at the old table as Anne came in from the kitchen carrying a large tray on which were the four biggest steaks Rowdy had ever seen. She was clad in a simple blue dress. Her long black hair, usually pinned back tightly in a bun, fell loosely about her shoulders. She smiled as she served out the steaks. Suddenly it felt good to be home.

"I hope you're hungry," she said.

"I most certainly am. I've missed your cooking," said Rowdy tucking into his steak. "This is superb. It tastes as good as it smells."

"Well thank you, kind sir," Anne replied making a mock curtsey. "It seems that Richmond has given you a soft tongue for flattery."

"Maybe so, but it didn't give me any fighting men."

"So your trip was a failure?" enquired Bill Lattimer.

"Well, I've been promised help but . . . "

Rowdy broke off as the remaining dinner guest entered the main room. It was not Dawn. Nevertheless, she was one of the most beautiful women he had ever seen. She had long, golden-blonde hair and soft blue eyes. When she smiled her whole face seemed to light up. She wore a black gown that was cut daringly low even by the standards of Richmond's high society.

"I'm so sorry I'm late," she said,

with a slight Southern accent.

"Not to worry. We've only just started, Helen," said Bill Lattimer as he stood up to greet her. "My dear, this is John's boy, Rod. Young man, let me introduce your stepmother's sister, Helen Forrester."

"So you're the famous Rowdy Carter. I expected somebody older. My late husband often spoke of you and I have followed your exploits ever since," said Helen in her most flattering way.

Her long, fluttering eyelashes, husky voice and affected breathlessness, were calculated to make the blood tingle in any man. Especially when followed up by extremely provocative eye contact, as in this case. Helen had spent hours putting on make-up, selecting precisely the right dress and rehearsing her entrance to achieve the effect she desired. Of course, she succeeded, but then she always had.

Startled, Rowdy jumped up to greet her. As he did so, Helen made a formal curtsey, knowing full well that from his vantage point her low-cut gown would reveal most of her ample breasts. She was no longer young but at thirty-five, Helen Forrester was in the full bloom of her womanhood and knew how to exploit every last bit of her femininity, and when the moment was right, she intended to do so. Helen needed to be alone with Rowdy before Dawn returned to tell her side of the story. Once alone with Rowdy, she intended to spin her special web of magic. After all he was only another man, however famous. Once she had created the right circumstances she was confident that she could get what she wanted. Had she not always done so with every man she had ever met?

Conversation over dinner mainly concerned the progress made in refurbishing the ranch. It seemed that Bill Lattimer had worked wonders during Rowdy's absence. Although Bill Lattimer had only succeeded in hiring Tom Handy and his son, Clem, both of them had worked non-stop ever since they had moved into the bunkhouse. Most of the work that needed to be done had been completed. The new responsibility had rejuvenated Bill and he looked years younger. Still unaware of his father's murder, Rowdy decided to ask him to hire Bill permanently to run the ranch. Then Anne might be persuaded to live on the ranch when she was not teaching in Clearwater. The ranch house could easily be extended to include them both. It would have to be enlarged anyway, if one distant day he was to return on a permanent basis.

Helen said little during dinner. She was not ready to discuss her future with Rowdy especially as Anne's eyes never left him for a second. Instead, Helen busied herself clearing the dishes, graciously refusing Anne's offer of help.

"No dear, you and Rowdy have some catching up to do. You don't want little old outsider me eavesdropping. I'll do the dishes and make the coffee while you just talk your heads off.

Perhaps when Captain Carter has a little spare time, we can talk over my little problem? Sometime tomorrow perhaps?"

Helen, like the rest of them, had no way of knowing about Rowdy's promotion in the new US Cavalry. Without waiting for a reply she glided off into the kitchen, leaving the heady aroma of her exotic perfume behind. She was pleased with the way she had already begun to turn the situation to her advantage. True to her word she washed all the dishes and made a large pot of coffee. While she busied herself in the kitchen, she smiled to herself contentedly. Tomorrow she would persuade Rowdy to take her riding and begin to work on him. She needed to stay at the ranch and get rid of Dawn. She realized that Anne was besotted with Rowdy but Helen was confident that she could handle that situation. After all, she thought, what could a prim schoolteacher know about love-making?

Unknown to her husband, Helen had enjoyed many lovers during the war. After his sudden death, under very suspicious circumstances, there had been many politicians only too anxious to console her. She had refused none of them, willingly acting out their wildest fantasies. There had been nothing that she wouldn't do, provided that her lovers had been prepared to meet her price for their pleasures.

Rowdy did not continue the conversation after Helen went into the kitchen. He was exhausted after his dam-busting activities of the previous night and turned in early. As he climbed into bed he decided that in the morning he would ride to Bottom Creek and check how much water had flowed down from the dam. He hoped that Anne would ride with him until he remembered that she had to return to Clearwater to teach in the little school. Perhaps if Dawn had not returned, Helen might like to see the results of his handiwork? The ride might give her the chance to discuss her problems, whatever they were.

The overnight rain-clouds dispersed in the heat of the morning sun so, by the time Rowdy had finished breakfast, the sky was bright blue. The weekend over, Anne had already started on her way to Clearwater to teach at the school. It was the last few days of term and soon she would be free to return full-time to Triple Creek to help her father run the ranch. Now that Rowdy was back she was looking forward to that more than she cared to admit, even though she heartily disliked Helen. Anne bitterly resented Helen for the way she had led on her father and the way she now looked at Rowdy.

Dawn had also disliked her aunt from the moment that she had unexpectedly arrived at Triple Creek. Her aunt had failed to give any explanation for her abrupt departure from New Orleans. Instead, she had used her charms to flatter Bill Lattimer. Much to Dawn's dismay and Anne's disquiet, he had invited her to stay. From that moment,

Helen proceeded to take charge, even though Triple Creek was Dawn's home. In the continued absence of her father, Dawn felt strongly that she should be in charge of the ranch, yet Helen treated her worse than a slave. When the two of them were alone, Helen criticized everything Dawn did. In the presence of Bill she was as nice as she could be to her niece. Dawn could not cope with Helen's abrupt change of manner and continued to be antagonistic towards her aunt, making it look as if she was the guilty party. Dawn's past reputation for having a sharp tongue and a fiery temper went against her.

In an attempt to bring peace back to the ranch, Anne suggested that Dawn might like to spend the weekends at the Lattimers' house while Anne spent the time with her father at Triple Creek. Dawn jumped at the chance. Helen, acting out the part of the injured party, offered to take over the household chores at the weekend. In fact, Anne did most of them. So, in spite of Dawn's earlier insistence to Rowdy that she would never leave Triple Creek, she found that she had already started the process. Helen had in a few days achieved more than all the Lazy K gunmen had done in months. That was why Major Norton paid her so highly. He never left anything to chance. Paying his former mistress to spy on Triple Creek was just another example of the man's thoroughness and attention to detail.

Unaware of Helen Forrester's true role, Rowdy agreed to take her on a picnic to Bottom Creek. Helen proved to be a competent rider, even though she rode side-saddle, much to the amusement of Black Bart. If only he could persuade his master to ride like that he would soon show which of them was really the master. However, Black Bart had no such luck. He had to content himself by showing his annoyance at again being parted from the pack-mule. He pranced, snorted loudly and tossed his head in defiance.

As usual, his master simply ignored his antics.

Apart from the food, Helen came well prepared for the picnic. She had made it her business to find out about the childhood feud between Dawn and Rowdy and planned to use it to her advantage. She well knew the effect that she had on men and had chosen her special white blouse to go with her black leather riding outfit. The blouse was modest enough in appearance but she had removed its original buttons and replaced them with smaller ones. As a result the slightest pressure on the blouse caused it to fly open. It was a trick she had used to her advantage several times, but today she was playing for high stakes, so deliberately wore nothing under her blouse.

After all, Rowdy was quite famous. Not everyone had a novel named after them, no matter how trashy and inaccurate it was. She had wheedled out of Bill Lattimer that Rowdy was rich and had paid off the mortgage of

Triple Creek. She had also discovered that only half of the ranch would be Rowdy's after his father's death. Dawn would inherit the other half. It was clear even to Helen, more accustomed to life in Richmond and latterly, New Orleans, that Triple Creek could be made into a prosperous concern. Always providing that it didn't fall into the hands of Major Norton.

If Rowdy won, there was no way that Helen was going to let him share it with Dawn. Helen wanted all of the ranch profits to herself, and Rowdy as well, at least until she tired of him. Why not, she thought? Stranger marriages had happened. On the other hand should the major win, she would only have been doing what he had paid her to do; that is, spy on the occupants of Triple Creek.

No matter who won, Dawn had to go. Not only because she stood to inherit half of Triple Creek but because she might contact relatives in New Orleans. They would certainly tell her about the notorious life Helen had led and the scandal that had finally caused her to leave that great city in such a hurry. Worse still, almost certainly they would inform the authorities where Helen was staying. In that case she knew that she would spend the rest of her life in the state prison. Not that her stay in prison would likely be a very long one: the authorities in New Orleans had no compunction about hanging a woman for murder, especially when the victim had been her husband.

She shivered at the thought and put down the leg of chicken she had been eating. Rowdy mistook the reason for the shiver as a dark cloud temporarily blotted out the sun's warmth. He stretched across her in order to put his jacket round her shoulders. It was the moment Helen had been waiting for and she clicked into well-rehearsed action.

At first she moved closer to Rowdy and snuggled into him. Then just as Rowdy's arms were draping his coat around her, she suddenly jerked backwards, twisting sharply away from him. Deliberately overbalancing, she grabbed Rowdy and pulled him down on top of her. Her sudden gyrations produced the desired effect. Her blouse flew open as most of its buttons gave up their unequal struggle to stay done up. Startled and embarrassed, Rowdy struggled to pull away.

Helen, still lying flat on her back, smiled beguilingly. It had all been so easy. Now she had got him where she wanted him. So, before he could recover, she put her hands behind his neck and pulled herself up. To her great satisfaction as she did so, she revealed the rest of her breasts that had remained covered by her half-open blouse.

"Why Rowdy, I am surprised," she said in mock indignation. "We hardly know each other. Never mind, my dear, I can't think of a better way to get acquainted."

She pulled him down on top of her and kissed him passionately. She wanted him desperately. So much so that she had to restrain herself from removing the rest of her garments. She told herself it must be a little more each time, until she was sure he was completely hooked. Even so, had he tried to make love to her, she would have let him. She was disappointed when he pulled away without attempting to disrobe her further but recovered her composure rapidly. She felt elated all the way back to the ranch. This time she actually liked the feel of this man as he touched her and that made a pleasant change. Nevertheless, for a little while she would hold back and let Rowdy get over his surprise. Like a prize salmon, she would play him on the end of her line, letting him run free but with the hook in his mouth. Tomorrow, she would smile at him and show that she was not angry. Then a few days later, she would lead him on again. Only when she was sure she had him where she wanted him, would they become lovers. No man had ever rejected her love-making. By having both Rowdy and the major as her lovers, Helen felt that she would be wealthy very soon.

Rowdy, on the other hand, did not recover his composure as quickly. The episode had awakened the guilt feelings he had felt after making love to his stepmother. But were they the same feelings of guilt? No, he decided, they were not. He was no longer the innocent ranch boy who had once been seduced. It wasn't his father he was betraying, nor was it Anne. Although he was still very fond of her, he seemed to have overcome his boyhood infatuation. So why did he feel like he did? He didn't know and anyway there were more important things to concentrate on than his love life. He tried to anticipate what the Lazy K would do next but their move had already been made. His father and Jack Denton lay dead in the Wastelands, murdered by the hired guns of Major Norton.

8

MAJOR NORTON was pleased with the results of Rex Morden's foul handiwork. Both men who could have got in the way of his plans had been eliminated. However, he might still need an alibi for the shootings, so he decided to take the long way back to Clearwater via Fort Smith. Whilst there he would make his presence known by buying something and obtaining a bill of sale for it. Then, when he returned to Clearwater, he could prove that he had not been anywhere near the Wastelands should he be accused of the murders.

Even the news of Rowdy's return did not unduly trouble the major. What could one man do against him? Nothing. Rowdy Carter, in spite of his reputation, was helpless without the help of hired guns. The major was confident that the only guns for hire were already on his payroll.

He was only half right in his assumption, for he had overlooked one important fact: not every gun was for hire to the highest bidder. Even as the major set out for Fort Smith, echoes from his lurid past were returning to haunt him. Men who lived by the gun and had little else in common except their hatred for the major were making their separate ways to Clearwater.

Bob Denton was the nearest. Although he had encountered the major during the war he was, as yet, unaware that he had bought the Lazy K. As Bob paused by the water-hole, trouble was the last thing on his mind. It had been a surprisingly hot day for spring and there was still a long way to go. Long in time, if not in actual distance, to the Running Dog ranch. After all these years, Bob Denton was not returning to his brother's ranch empty-handed. Unaware of his brother's death he had bought him a gift. It was this gift that was causing Bob to make such slow progress in returning home.

Like his boyhood friend, Rowdy, Bob had gone to the war, only he had chosen to fight for the North; but like Rowdy, he had not returned home when the hostilities ceased. Instead, he had joined one of the first cattle drives out of Texas. Then he became a sheriff and finally a deputy US marshal.

Bob had called his brother's gift, Angus. You only had to glance at him to see why. Angus was no ordinary bull: he was a giant, much heavier and far tougher than even the biggest of the shorthorn bulls. These were being specially imported from England for breeding purposes but they were dwarfed by the mighty Angus. His ancestry went back to the rugged Highlands of Scotland. There, the wickedly pointed horns of his forefathers had fought off packs of hungry wolves and even dealt with the bears that had once roamed the Highlands. They were far hardier than their English counterparts, their long black hair enabling them to withstand the worst blizzards of the Scottish winter.

Angus was as dangerous as any buffalo, yet he followed Bob like a puppy. He had done so ever since Bob had found him on a deserted ranch almost two months ago. It was finding Angus that had prompted Bob to return home. In any case, he had tired of the life of a gun-fighter. Since he had become a deputy marshal, twelve men had tried unsuccessfully to match the speed of their draw against his. Bob's fast draw had consigned them all to Boot Hill, but as his reputation grew, so had the number of challenges. Quick as he was on the draw, there were faster. So it could only be a matter of time before he met his match. He intended to return home and retire before the inevitable happened. He wanted to cross-breed Angus with the cows on the Running Dog ranch. By this means he hoped to produce a larger, more durable steer, better able to cope with the hazards of a trail-drive.

Bob's day-dream was interrupted by Angus. The great beast finished drinking and slowly moved on towards the Running Dog ranch. It was almost as if the great beast had read Bob's thoughts and approved them, especially when it came to the part about mating.

* * *

A hundred miles behind Bob and the massive Angus another rider moved slowly nearer to Clearwater. He was a huge man who looked slightly comical as he rode a burro not much larger than Rowdy's pack-mule. Like many from the South, he wore no shoes because he could not afford them. During the war he served as a corporal with Sergeant Browne. His commanding officer had been Rowdy Carter. After the war Jed Pickett had tried his best to settle down and be a dirt-farmer even though he disliked it. He tried because that was what the love of his life had wanted him to do — the love of his life who had died in childbirth because he had no money for a doctor; no money because their meagre crops had been destroyed by riders as they fled across his lands. Later, Jed found out that the leader of the riders was a disgraced major by the name of Norton. So, when word of Rowdy's troubles with the same Major Norton reached him from his old sergeant, Jed left his little daughter with friends, packed up his belongings and rode off to help his old commanding officer.

As he left, Jed vowed to himself that his little daughter would want for nothing. His Bowie knife would see to that. During the war, the Union had laid waste the plantations of his boyhood. Even now most of the Shenandoah Valley was still in ruin or, worse still in Jed's eyes, in the hands of Yankees. Jed had vowed he would never work for any Yankee. Otherwise he might have been an overseer, then he might have had enough money for a doctor to save his beloved wife.

Major Norton had simply been the last of a long line of Yankees who had helped to ruin Jed's life. Jed's preacher had instructed him to pray for the Yankees and forgive them for their wrong-doings. He could not, but he swore that he would do the next best thing. Using his Bowie knife, he was only too willing to send as many Yankees as he could to their Maker so they could ask His forgiveness in person. The preacher had often told him how much more difficult it was for a rich man to enter Heaven than it was for a poor man. So Jed saw it as his duty to take their money before dispatching any Yankees to that most exalted of holy places. He would not harm anyone from the South but he had robbed three Yankees before sending them to meet their Maker. In Jed's eyes, a good Christian could do no less. He sent all the money he stole to the folks looking after his daughter.

★ ★ ★

A day's hard riding behind Jed Pickett, his old sergeant gave the orders for his young troopers to dismount. Ellis Browne carried sealed orders for his new major, but they would have to wait a little longer. In spite of the heat, his young troopers still proudly wore their new blue coats. They had yet to learn that a fresh horse and a canteen full of water were their most vital possessions. A supply of water was even more important for the horses than it was for the troopers. Their eventual destination was wild and full of hostile Indians, so keeping their horses fresh could well make the difference between surviving to fight another day or losing their scalps.

Sergeant Ellis took hold of his horse's reins and began to lead it. The rest of the troopers did the same, following in single line exactly as they had been trained. The sergeant smiled to himself. His young troopers were as green as grass. They were finding that it was one thing to do well during training but on this deserted trail, the going was far harder than they expected.

Unfortunately, the trail only appeared to be deserted. Although they were unaware of it, every move they made was being closely observed by less than friendly eyes. The major had spies everywhere.

"Give us a song," ordered the sergeant oblivious to the hostile eyes watching from the shadows. "A cheerful one, mind. A song to make the next few miles pass quicker."

The troopers began to sing 'When Johnny Comes Marching Home'. It was a song from the Civil War which they all enjoyed. It no longer belonged to one side but now united those it once divided. Spirits still high, the young troopers sang loudly, oblivious to all around them.

Some distance away, two horsemen drew rein and paused. The sound of the troopers singing completely masked them and their two spare horses, not only from the troopers, but from the major's men, spying on them. The two riders were quick to spot the gunmen trailing the troopers. Frank turned and looked quizzically at his brother.

"What do you make of it?" he asked.

"I don't know," his brother admitted. "Those bluecoats look as if they're still wet behind the ears. They haven't seen us or the men shadowing them."

"But why should anyone out here want to spy on the bluecoats?" asked Frank.

"It's a mystery, Frank, and you know I don't like mysteries," replied his brother. "I think we should tail them and see what happens."

The battle-seasoned veterans of the Civil War had no difficulty in turning the table, and the spies became the spied upon. They had left Clearwater to return to their gang, but only to share out the loot from their last train robbery. Reward posters for their capture were everywhere, so it was time for the gang to split up. Some of the gang had decided to settle down. Before the brothers could do that, they had a debt of honour to pay. Now that they were sure Norton was behind the murder of their relatives, revenge was their reason for returning to Clearwater. However, their revenge was going to have to wait until they found out why the troopers were being tailed.

* * *

Kital was the first of the travellers to reach Triple Creek. As the old Indian had guessed, Dawn was desolated by the murder of her stepfather. Rowdy felt numbed, while the one-handed Bill Lattimer felt more helpless than ever. Kital left as soon as he had delivered the tragic news. He went to seek the solitude of the Indian Mountains to mourn, in private, the loss of his old friend.

The sad news forced Helen to delay her plans of Rowdy's conquest, so she willingly became the shoulder for them all to cry on, a role she played with considerable skill, insidiously playing on the grief of her companions as she weaved her way deeper and deeper into their confidence. Soon Helen knew all there was to know about Triple Creek and the aspirations of those who occupied it. Information she meant to put to good use at the right moment. Even so, she was impatient to return to her conquest of Rowdy, although there was little she could do about that for the moment.

With the return of Dawn and Anne to Triple Creek, the crowding of the relatively small ranch house was a problem. It was temporarily solved by Rowdy moving back into his old quarters in the bunkhouse. However, whilst this allowed Rowdy to get away from the attentions of Helen, it created a potentially serious problem: the new sleeping arrangements meant that in the event of a surprise night attack, the occupants of the ranch house would be poorly protected. Whilst both Dawn and Anne were fair shots with a rifle and Bill still had Rowdy's shotgun, they would not be able to withstand a raid by professional gunmen.

Unfortunately, Rowdy was kept too busy to sort out this problem. He was obliged to spend the next few days in town sorting out the legal affairs of the ranch. He was also obliged to inform the bank of the death of Jack Denton. At first, its manager, Barnabus Reno, did nothing. Rowdy correctly deduced he was waiting for orders. The day after Major Norton returned, Reno announced that due to the death of Jack Denton, the bank would have to call in the mortgage on the Running Dog. Unless it was paid within ten days, the ranch would be put up for auction. Since nobody in Clearwater had the amount of money necessary to bid for a ranch the size of the Running Dog, it seemed that Major Norton would be able to purchase the ranch cheaply. However, Rowdy had other ideas.

* * *

The major sat in the huge lounge of the Lazy K's Mexican-style ranch house, confident that everything was going smoothly. Buying the Running Dog with the money taken from the dead body of its owner was a bonus. Rowdy's action in destroying the dams at Hawks Ridge, far from hindering his plans, had actually helped him. Once the Running Dog ranch was his, he would have had to destroy both dams anyway. Self-satisfied, he contentedly puffed on his cheroot. Yet, as he poured out another glass of brandy, events were already beginning to conspire against him as, one by one, the travellers began to arrive.

Bob Denton was the first. Unaware of his brother's murder, the last surviving Denton was shocked to find the Running Dog ranch deserted. Only a few chickens clucked in alarm as Bob wandered around the empty buildings. The whole ranch appeared neglected and the once fertile pastures of the ranch were dry and dusty brown. It was a most disappointing homecoming. Finally, Bob decided to head for Triple Creek. He began to fear the worst; it was very unlike his brother to leave the ranch unattended.

As there was no pasture for Angus to graze, Bob took the mighty beast with him. Angus roared his displeasure. He had been on the trail for weeks and needed to rest. He wanted to graze on lush meadow grass, drink fresh water and find a herd of cows to satisfy his mating lust. However, there was nothing of interest on this deserted ranch, so once again the great beast followed his new master.

★ ★ ★

Back in Clearwater, it had been another quiet day. Business in the whorehouse had been very slack. Major Norton had ordered his gunmen to stay out of town until he had completed the purchase of the Running Dog ranch. Rowdy had finished his business with the bank. After ordering more provisions from the store to be picked up on his next visit, he returned to Triple Creek.

So an hour later, the streets were almost deserted as Jed Pickett rode into the town. The giant looked ridiculous perched on top of his tiny burro, but no one even smiled. One look at Jed and his big Bowie knife discouraged any such notion. He dismounted by the hardware store and went in. Used to walking barefoot, the stony street caused him little discomfort.

"Looking for a friend. Is the Carter ranch nearby?" Jed asked the portly storekeeper.

"A fair ride, especially on a burro,"

172

replied the storekeeper.

"Anything wrong with my burro?" asked Jed angrily.

"Hell, no. You say you're looking for a friend?" said the fat storekeeper, hastily changing the subject.

"Rowdy Carter. Served under him in the Virginian Irregulars."

The mention of Rowdy's name brought a smile to the storekeeper's face. He was genuinely pleased to see anyone who was a friend of Rowdy's, especially when they were from the South. They discussed conditions in Virginia over several pipes of the storekeeper's best tobacco. The store-keeper had befriended Rowdy on the day he first returned to Clearwater and again went out of his way to help. He agreed to let Jed take a wagonload of provisions to Triple Creek. As there were no Lazy K gunmen in town to bother them, they had the wagon loaded in no time at all and Jed was soon on his way.

However, it was not Jed, but Bob

Denton who first reached Triple Creek. Black Bart saw him approaching leading a huge, black monster. The big stallion stopped grazing, then froze to the spot, as Bob opened the corral gate and ushered the beast in. Black Bart could not take his eyes off the long curved horns of Angus. Bob closed the corral gate, then made his way to the ranch house, leaving the huge black thing inside the corral. For the first time Black Bart felt afraid. Big as the black horse stood, this long-haired monster dwarfed him.

Angus merely glanced at Black Bart and dismissed him with complete contempt. The mighty bull had been walking for a very long time and here in the corral the alfalfa was lush, the water sweet. The insignificant black horse was unimportant; there was some serious grazing to be done. Then it would be time to sort out the pathetic little beasts that passed for bulls on this ranch. Once he had done that he could turn his attention to the many cows he could hear plaintively calling to him from the nearby pastures. Yes, the prospects looked good to the long-haired beast, this was to be home, the days of roaming were at an end.

Though he had not seen him for years, Bill Lattimer recognized Bob Denton instantly and came out of the ranch house to greet him. Bill was unaware that Bob did not know of his brother's death. Though it was only late afternoon, they both downed a generous glass of rye as they discussed the sad news. Bob was visibly shocked by the death of his brother and John Carter.

"Do you know who did it?" he asked.

"No, Bob. I suspect that Major Norton had a part in it, but as yet there's no real proof," replied the former sheriff of Clearwater.

"Norton! I didn't know he was here. That bas . . . "

Bob Denton broke off hastily as Anne and Helen entered the room from the kitchen. They had been helping Dawn to prepare the evening meal. As they sat down, Rowdy returned from Clearwater. He was delighted to see his childhood friend.

"It's good to see you, Bob. It's been a long time. Too bad it couldn't have been under better circumstances."

The evening meal was difficult for all, so conversation was very subdued. Bob's return had re-emphasized the feelings of bereavement caused by the deaths of John Carter and Jack Denton. The loss was felt keenly by all bar one sitting round the table. Helen was too preoccupied with her scheming to think about anything else. However, they had barely started to eat when they were interrupted by a shout from outside.

"Hello, you all in the house!"

Rowdy was first to the door, gun in hand. But to the surprise of the others, he burst out laughing.

"Well, well. I don't believe it. Who will turn up next?" he said in astonishment.

It was Jed Pickett in the supply wagon.

"Evening, Captain, come to see if you needed a hand. Don't mind what I do except taking orders from a Yankee. Seems to me that we've met before," said Jed, staring hard at Bob Denton.

He had, Bob had been in the Battle of Harpers Creek. Following the Union victory, he had been one of many who had put the Shenandoah Valley to the torch. During that time he had been involved in several unsuccessful skirmishes against General Mosby's men, one of which had contained Rowdy and the giant Jed Pickett. Jed's hatred for anything to do with the Union was plain to see, so Bob merely shook his head and declined to answer further.

Rowdy was both delighted and astonished to see one of his old troop. He knew Jed to be both cool and resourceful under fire and immediately offered the big man a job on the ranch. With the arrival of Jed Pickett the sides were almost complete. Conflict was now inevitable as the seeds of range war were sown. It remained to be seen which side, if any, the brothers would take. Only one thing was certain, of all the gunmen being drawn to Clearwater, Frank's brother was by far the most deadly. Anybody standing in his way would not live long.

9

TWO days before the date set by the bank for the redemption of the Running Dog mortgage, Rowdy rode into Clearwater in the supply wagon. He was accompanied by Helen Forrester. It had been agreed that she would move into the Lattimers' house until Bill Lattimer had finished supervising the rebuilding of the derelict barn. Rowdy left a very unhappy black stallion in the corral it still shared with Angus. The huge beast continued to ignore Black Bart but had struck up a good relationship with the pack-mule, adding further to the misery of the horse.

Clearwater was quiet, the Lazy K gunmen had not yet been allowed into the town. Rowdy dropped Helen at the Lattimers' house and carried in her luggage. Though she had left most of it at Triple Creek, she had still brought a trunk full of clothes. He left Helen to unpack and headed towards the bank. On the way he noticed several scantily clad harlots brazenly strutting in front of the whorehouse trying to drum up trade. Rowdy ignored them and continued straight to the bank.

Once inside, he was ushered into the manager's office. He was greeted with the obsequious reverence that Barnabus Reno reserved for the very wealthy. It was far cry from his first visit to the bank when, dressed as a Confederate drifter, he had been treated with contempt. However, this meeting was to be no less contentious than the first. Rowdy tipped most of the gold coins from his other saddle-bag on to the manager's desk, then outlined his proposition. Reno's face turned white as he listened. Torn between accepting the consequences of Rowdy's offer or losing the gold, Reno was reduced to pleading.

"Surely you see that if I do as you

ask, Mr Carter, the bank could be faced with very serious repercussions," he said, as beads of sweat began to form on his brow.

"I see nothing of the sort. If you accept my proposal, the bank cannot lose financially. If you refuse, I shall not deposit the gold you see and I shall withdraw the rest I've already banked with you. Then I shall ensure that everybody is told that I have closed my account because your bank is in financial trouble."

"Mr Carter, you mustn't. That might start a run on the bank."

"Too bad, Barnabus, but why should I worry? I'll have my money," said Rowdy as he began to enjoy the plump bank manager's discomfort.

"But if you withdraw all your money, there won't be enough left to pay out everyone. Especially, if they all came at once. The bank has reserves, but it would take weeks to get the money here. By time it would be too late. The bank might even have to close!"

Reno shook at the idea. Panic showed on his fat face and he began to sweat even more. Remorselessly, Rowdy pressed home his advantage.

"I don't suppose the governors would look too kindly on a manager who allowed that sort of thing to happen, especially if they found out that it could have been avoided. You know, Barnabus, I have an odd feeling that someone would tell them, don't you?"

"Yes, Mr Carter, I'm sure you're right."

Sweat was pouring from the manager's brow as he replied. Rowdy judged he had frightened the man enough to get his way, so he continued in a more conciliatory tone.

"Lucky for you then, it doesn't have to be that way. Instead you can do a good business deal for the bank, make a good friend of me and the run on the bank will never happen."

"It seems that you leave me no choice," replied the panic-stricken manager. "But what about Major

Norton? He will be furious when he finds out."

"Probably, Barnabus, but then we can't please everyone, can we?"

The deal was struck and Rowdy left the bank pleased with the outcome. He made his way over to the store and picked up three boxes of the unusual .42 calibre ammunition for his Le Mat pistol. As promised, the storekeeper had ordered it specially for him. He also collected several boxes of buckshot, and various calibre bullets for the rest of the rifles and pistols. After loading the ammunition into the supply wagon, he drove back to the Lattimers' house. On the way, he passed a woman making her way to the saloon. She made several obscene remarks, leaving Rowdy in no doubt that she would do anything he wanted for the right sum of money. He ignored her and rode on.

Helen waited impatiently for Rowdy to return. Once she had him alone in the Lattimers' house she was certain she would be able to seduce him. Then he would be under her spell. She was confident that he would prove little different to the many men she had bedded. First, she would lead him on again, then make him wait a few days until he begged for more. She would do this in spite of her own desperate desire for him. Helen knew that she could always satisfy her lust with Major Norton. She knew that the major was sure to visit her as soon as he discovered that she had moved into Clearwater. The seclusion of the Lattimers' house would make it easy to make both the major and Rowdy her lovers. Then, no matter which of them proved to be the victor, he would be hers. More to the point, so would the victor's wealth.

She had thought she had only a short time to open up the house before Rowdy returned. Certainly not long enough to unpack and change into one of her elaborate and sexy costumes. So she simply unbuttoned the front of her pink blouse in readiness for him.

However, he seemed to be taking much longer than she expected.

Though Rowdy had told her the nature of the business transaction he intended to complete at the bank, he had not mentioned that he was going to the store to collect ammunition. In spite of the unbuttoned state of her blouse, Helen peered out of the window to see whether he was coming. As she did, Major Norton rode down the road towards the saloon. Fortunately his attention was focused on another rider heading towards him. Although Helen had never seen the second rider before, she recognized him at once from Anne's description of him. It was Rex Morden.

Suddenly, both riders broke into a gallop and disappeared down the side road behind the whorehouse, much to the disappointment of the harlots waiting in front of it. The dust stirred up by the riders' horses had not settled when Rowdy appeared driving the supply wagon.

Helen guessed that it would not take the major long to find out that she had moved into town, his spies were everywhere. That being so he was certain to pay her a visit before he left town. If he came while Rowdy was visiting, the consequences for her could only be disastrous. Quickly she rebuttoned her blouse as she waited for Rowdy. She decided to warn him about the presence of the major and Morden, then try to persuade him to leave town. He could always return one evening unseen under the cover of darkness. By then she would be better prepared and she should be able to persuade Rowdy to stay all night.

Rowdy needed little persuasion to leave town immediately. He was very well aware of Helen's allure, but had no real desire to become sexually involved with her. He told himself that it would be too much like reliving the affair with his stepmother. However, that wasn't the real reason, but he wasn't ready to admit it.

Only a few minutes after Rowdy left, Rex Morden rapped the front door of the Lattimers' cottage. He had come to show Anne his new sheriff's badge. He was surprised when Helen Forrester and not Anne opened the door, though his air of belligerence changed as Helen explained her long-standing relationship with the major — a torrid relationship that had led to the murder of her husband, but she kept that part of it to herself. Rex Morden left and rode straight to the major. A few minutes later the major arrived only to be kept waiting as she again readjusted her blouse. The major was pleased to see her but he got straight down to business.

"Rex tells me that you have news from Triple Creek and why Carter visited the bank."

Without answering him, Helen disappeared into the kitchen. She knew how to handle the major. She remained in the kitchen as she called out to him, "Yes, my dear, I'll tell you all their plans in a while. First there's something much more important we must do."

"What could be more important than our future, Helen?"

Instead of replying, Helen walked back into the parlour. She didn't say a word, but the major had his answer. This time she hadn't merely undone her blouse, she had removed it completely. She stood before him, naked to the waist.

"You can take the rest of my clothes off. Right now! Unless you still want to talk business. In that case I'll get dressed again, my dear."

But she didn't have to. In fact by the time Helen got out of bed and put her clothes back on, Rowdy had reached the Triple Creek ranch. She thought of him all the time she was making love to the major yet that did not prevent her from enjoying every second of it. Neither did her erotic thoughts of Rowdy prevent her from telling the major all she had found out at Triple Creek and the deal Rowdy had just completed with the bank. The major's fury at the news spurred on his passion as Helen hoped that it would. However, it was the occupants of Triple Creek who were to feel the full effect of Helen's treachery.

10

IT was the scale of the attack that caught Rowdy by surprise. As the first rays of the morning sun lit the sky, ten horsemen thundered into Triple Creek. They opened fire as soon as they came into range. Rowdy, awakened by the gunfire, cursed himself for leaving the house guarded only by Bill Lattimer.

The renegades dismounted and rushed the ranch house, knowing that it was poorly defended. Helen's treachery was about to cost its occupants dearly. The attackers stormed into the house but not without loss. Bill Lattimer fired both barrels of the shotgun Rowdy had loaned him. The effect at close range was devastating. Two outlaws were blasted into pulp by the buckshot. Handicapped by the loss of his right hand, Bill was unable to reload before he was struck down by a hail of bullets. He died instantly.

It was all over in a few seconds. The leader of the outlaws, Warlock Sims, stood in the main room and reviewed the situation. His scarred face broke into a satisfied smile. It had been all too easy. The ranch house had been captured for the loss of only two men, both easily replaced. He bound, then gagged Dawn and Anne. Capturing the two girls was an added bonus. The renegade leader knew that his boss, Major Norton, would pay a handsome price for them. The two women were both good lookers. The sight of them, bound and helpless, excited his perverted lust.

Warlock Sims was a small man, just over thirty years old. He dressed in the uniform of a dragoon officer and his men addressed him as colonel, although Sims had never been an officer. During the Civil War he had been a guard in a Union transit camp where Southern prisoners, mostly civilians, had been exchanged for Unionists detained in the South. Even then his perverted carnal lust had got him into trouble. His commanding officer had interrupted Sims in the middle of one of his more sadistic sexual attacks on one of the women prisoners. Sims had shot him and deserted, but not before raiding the commanding-officer's quarters and stealing his spare uniform. Sims still wore the uniform, even though it had been several years since the incident occurred.

Warlock Sims did not wear a holster, but tucked in a sash round his waist was a Bowie knife and one of the new Colt .45 revolvers. He wore it butt first and was fast, very fast. He killed for the sheer pleasure of it. That's why men like Major Norton hired him. His tally was fifteen dead, not including the women he had butchered with his Bowie knife during his frenzies of perverted lust. He gazed longingly at the two defenceless women and thought that he would add one, if not both, to his score before this job was over.

Whilst Sims was pondering over the fate of Dawn and Anne, Rowdy led the occupants of the bunkhouse across the open ground to the barn. The swiftness of the move took Sims and his renegades by surprise. As a result, they fired only a few harmless shots before Rowdy and the rest of his group reached the safety of the barn. The move puzzled Sims, for the barn offered no strategic value to Rowdy. Nothing much happened for several minutes. Then the five men, riding at full gallop, suddenly appeared from behind the barn. This time Sims had his men primed and ready for any type of attack. He needn't have bothered. The riders turned away from the house and galloped towards the Indian Mountains.

"They're giving up without a fight," yelled an exultant Warlock Sims.

When he was sure that the riders were not going to turn back Sims turned away from the window. He pulled out his Bowie knife and slashed the ropes binding Anne. Then he grabbed savagely at the top of her dress. Anne screamed, fearing he was about to rape her. This time she was mistaken. Sims dragged her to the window and forced her to look at the retreating riders.

"See for yourself, girlie! Your precious Captain Carter runs like a frightened dog from Warlock Sims."

Anne watched until the riders disappeared from sight. Her silence made Dawn believe that Sims' taunting words were true and Rowdy had deserted them. Unlike Anne, Dawn was unaware of the role Rowdy had played during the Civil War. So she had no way of knowing that he would never put his own safety before hers. She bit back the tears, knowing they would only add to her captors' enjoyment.

A lone rider watched Rowdy and the rest gallop away. When he was certain they were not coming back, he approached the ranch house. It was

Rex Morden. Five minutes later he was locked in argument with Warlock Sims over the fate of the captured women.

"The women must not be harmed. At least, not until the major has seen them," said Morden firmly.

"But I only want a little fun. Look, I'll go shares with you. You can have first choice. Which one do you want, the redhead or the schoolteacher? I don't mind, as long as we swop over."

"No dice, Sims. Well, not until the major gets what he wants from them. Then we will see."

"What's the major want with them? Still never mind, I can wait. I don't much care who has them first, so long as I get my turn."

Rex was well aware of Sims' perverted sex lust. He wanted Anne for himself, but he knew that if he showed any interest in her, Sims would go for her first. That was part of Sims' perversion; taking women away from their men merely added to his sick enjoyment. Even if Anne survived the ordeal, Rex knew that he wouldn't want what was left, so pretended not to be interested.

"It's strictly business as far as the major's concerned, besides he's got Helen Forrester. That's more than he can handle by all accounts. Real hot stuff that one; from what I've been told, there isn't anything she won't do."

"Is she that good?" asked Warlock Sims, his lips almost drooling with anticipated pleasure.

"So the major says. As to these two, I don't mind just so long as I get one of them before you get your hands on her."

"It's not my hands they need to worry about," laughed Sims as he patted his large Bowie knife.

Sims put on an act of good humour towards Morden. He needed the gunman as an ally until he got paid. After that it didn't matter a damn. He had marked Anne for his special treatment. If Morden objected so much the better, Sims hadn't been fooled for a second: he knew that Morden wanted Anne for himself. Sims also added Helen Forrester to his list of women earmarked for his special attention. He was going to enjoy showing the major how to deal with a lusty woman.

Locked in the bedroom, Anne and Dawn overheard every word. They looked at each other in horror as they heard of Helen's relationship with Major Norton. They shivered at the thought of what the future held for them. They were scared by the prospect of facing Major Norton, but that was better than being left with the depraved Warlock Sims. So the girls offered little resistance when Morden ordered them into the old chuck-wagon and escorted them to the Lazy K. Sims seethed with frustrated rage, but did nothing to stop them leaving.

Anne and Dawn did everything they could to slow up the trip, hoping against hope that they would be rescued, but the trail remained deserted. When they finally arrived at the Lazy K, they were relieved to find that the major was in Clearwater. However, they were locked in a store-room until he returned.

* * *

The major had intended to return to his ranch straight after he had completed his business in Clearwater, but he was hungry, so first he headed for the saloon. This was much to the approval of the women who conducted their business there. Although the saloon was most certainly a brothel, it served the best steaks in town. The major was very partial to steak, and afterwards he might just find time to enjoy the pleasures offered by one of the saloon whores.

As he reached the saloon, the major saw Helen in the distance. She walked slowly towards the Lattimers' house. Dressed in a very fashionable white gown and carrying a pink parasol, she looked very becoming. She was far and away more alluring than any of the saloon whores. He knew that soon she would have to be eliminated. In her own way she was quite ruthless. At any time it suited her, she could expose him as the mastermind behind the attack on the Triple Creek and the murder of her husband. So very soon he planned to turn her over to the sadistic Warlock Sims. However, for the moment, he could safely enjoy the many pleasures of her willing and luscious body. He turned away from the saloon and hurried after her. His hunger, the saloon whores and the need to return to his ranch, completely forgotten.

★ ★ ★

Rowdy, on the other hand, had not forgotten the need to return to his ranch. He had to strike back hard at the renegades holding Triple Creek. Yet as long as the girls were held prisoner, force was out of the question. So, instead of storming the ranch house he led his men to the barn and collected some of the ammunition he had stored there. The rest he hid under the straw. Then, using the side of the barn to provide cover, they made their escape. Rowdy planned to set up his headquarters in the deserted Running Dog ranch and use it as a base from which he could counter-attack.

Unfortunately, the Running Dog was no longer deserted. Nor was Rowdy the only one who had planned in vain to use it as a hideout. The outlaw brothers, tired of trailing the bluecoats and the major's men spying on them, turned their attention to the Running Dog ranch. They were surprised to see that the once deserted ranch was now a hive of activity.

"I thought you said the ranch was deserted?" said Frank's brother.

"It was when I last rode through here. Seems like the Lazy K have taken it over since then."

One of the spare horses, a young grey

mare, whinnied loudly. The unsaddled horses in the Running Dog's corral whinnied back. Two of the gunmen by the bunkhouse stopped what they were doing and stared towards the thicket where the brothers were hiding. After a slight hesitation they called into the bunkhouse. After a few seconds, the rest of the gunmen rushed out.

"Frank! That damned filly of yours will be the death of us if you don't train her out of calling to every stallion she sees. Come on, let's get the hell out of here!"

Without replying, Frank gathered up the reins of the spare horses and galloped away from the ranch. His brother followed. A few seconds later all that was left of the brothers was the dust kicked up by their horses. Then a heated argument broke out amongst the Lazy K gunmen over which of them should saddle up and ride after the strangers.

If the gunmen had not been so engrossed in their argument they would not have been caught off guard by Rowdy and his raiders. Too late, they noticed the raiders as they galloped straight at them, guns drawn. Although the back of a galloping horse is not the ideal shooting platform, the raiders let loose a deadly salvo. Three gunmen died before the rest could respond. The survivors dived for the cover of the bunkhouse, but one more of them didn't make it.

The impetus of their charge took them past the bunkhouse and into range of the main ranch house. A hail of bullets flew too near the raiders for comfort, then a second barrage came from the bunkhouse. Though initially caught off guard, the gunmen had rapidly regrouped making further attack impossible. The raiders had inflicted heavy casualties, but failed in their objective to capture the ranch and turn it into their new base.

"Time to get out of here," yelled Rowdy.

"Too right," agreed Bob Denton as

a bullet whizzed perilously close to his ear.

In perfect unison the raiders wheeled around and raced away. They were long gone before the gunmen occupying the Running Dog could saddle up and follow them.

The raiders left four dead gunmen and another two wounded in the wake of their attack without suffering any injuries themselves. If Rowdy had been caught by surprise earlier that morning, then he had struck back with a vengeance. However, Bill Lattimer was dead, Dawn and Anne were still held captive and the enemy had gained possession of the Triple Creek and Running Dog ranches. So the first round of the range war had been won by the Lazy K.

11

THE bullet ricocheted against the boulder in front of him and whined harmlessly away. Sergeant Ellis Browne cursed under his breath. It wouldn't do to show his men that he was rattled. He hadn't seen the men shadowing them so he had led his troopers into the canyon and into a deadly trap. Ellis cursed softly to himself again. Too many days spent pushing paper at Richmond had made him soft and careless. Now they were pinned down by an unseen enemy, caught in a deadly crossfire from the canyon tops. So far he had lost one man and two horses, but the rest were relatively safe as long as they remained under cover of the protecting rocks.

Though it was still morning the canyon floor was already baking hot and the few canteens of water they had managed to salvage would not last long in the searing heat. The sergeant looked at his troopers. They were no more than boys, this was their first time under fire. He had ordered them to cease firing to conserve ammunition. Now each of them sat motionless behind one of the huge rocks that littered the canyon floor, calmly waiting for his next order. He gave none for their only hope was to do nothing until nightfall. Then they might crawl out of this death canyon on their bellies. Yet how many of them would be alive by nightfall? Precious few he thought.

Heavy firing broke out simultaneously from the top of both sides of the canyon. Between the broadsides the sergeant risked a glance over the top of his boulder. He ducked hastily as a fusillade of bullets struck the rocks around him. Yet he had seen enough. Covered by the barrage of protective fire from the cliff tops, at least half a dozen men were working their way down the ridge behind them. To fire at them meant exposing his men to the deadly hail of bullets from above. Without immediate help, Ellis Browne calculated that their life expectancy could be counted in minutes, the number of which could be counted on one hand. Luckily that help was about to arrive.

High on a bluff overlooking the canyon, two riders dispassionately watched the situation below them. They had returned from their unsuccessful mission to the Running Dog to find the bluecoats pinned down in the canyon by rifle fire. The two riders began a heated conversation.

"You're not thinking of helping the bluecoats are you, Brother?" said Frank, shocked at the idea of helping anyone in a blue uniform.

"Well, Frank, we have to go through the canyon to get to Clearwater, unless you want to ride through the Indian Mountains."

"No thanks," said Frank shaking his head.

Frank remembered all the stories he had heard about the Indian burial grounds. The Running Dog Indians were bad enough but the Apaches were even more dangerous. They also had some of their chiefs buried in the Indian Mountains and would never give up chasing any white man who had dared to set foot on the land they regarded as sacred.

"Right then, Frank," said his brother reaching for his carbine, "let's see if we can distract Major Norton's men long enough for the bluecoats to make a run for it."

* * *

The echo of their gunfire rolled around the hills. Nearby Rowdy signalled the raiders to stop their mad gallop away from the Running Dog ranch. For a moment all went quiet, then a few single shots were answered by a prolonged volley.

"What do you make of it?" asked Bob Denton.

"Sounds as if one or two guns are standing off a pack of gunmen," said Jed shrewdly. "But with all these blasted echoes I can't tell where the shots are coming from."

"Devil's Canyon," said Rowdy and Bob simultaneously.

It took barely fifteen minutes to reach the canyon. Black Bart, more like his old surly self the further away he galloped from Angus, suddenly became very excited. Even though he had been trained not to, he whinnied loudly. He had seen the pretty grey mare again.

Rowdy recognized the brothers instantly and saw that they had been trapped on the top of the bluff overlooking the canyon. The gunmen had mistakenly tried to rush them, as the bodies of four of them testified.

Silently the raiders fanned out and, carbines drawn, charged the outlaws. Caught on foot, the gunmen panicked and ran to their horses. It was their second error of judgement for which three more paid the ultimate penalty. The remainder reached their horses and rode rapidly away. The raiders were prevented from following by a shout from the top of the ridge.

"Bluecoats trapped on the canyon floor," called Frank.

Jed Pickett swore loudly but joined the others as they dismounted and crawled to the edge of the canyon. Sure enough, there were bluecoats trapped on the canyon floor. They looked in a bad way. At least three appeared to be dead. However, the raiders' appearance drew the fire from the outlaws on the other bank of the canyon. The raiders returned fire with a vengeance, pinning down the outlaws.

Sergeant Browne ordered his men to make a run for it. Leading his remaining troopers he sprinted across the open canyon floor to the surviving horses. Moments later they were galloping for their lives out of the canyon towards the Indian Mountains. A few minutes later Sergeant Browne reined in and dismounted. He looked around in dismay. Only two of his young troopers had survived.

★ ★ ★

The raiders saw the troopers, far below them, scramble madly for their horses. They increased their fire to cover them. Even so, one of the troopers crashed to the floor and failed to move again. When the rest of the troopers were well clear of the canyon, the raiders ceased firing and returned to their horses. They rode rapidly until out of range of the gunmen who were still on the opposite side of the canyon. Once safe, they paused to wait for the brothers to join them, then cantered towards the Indian Mountains.

Sergeant Ellis Browne saw the raiders approaching. Even though Rowdy was not in uniform, the surviving troopers stood to attention and saluted him.

"Good to see you, Major," said the sergeant.

"Glad we came along, but you should really thank these two," said Rowdy pointing at the brothers. "You would have been dead long before we arrived, if it hadn't been for them."

"Could we cut the reunion?" said Bob Denton. "We stand out like a sore thumb and I don't have enough ammunition left to fight off an angry gopher."

Frank's brother noted that Rowdy had been addressed as major not captain, something he intended to take up at a more suitable time. It was just a small thing, but his attention to apparently insignificant details had been one of the reasons he had remained alive for so long.

"Then I suggest that we make for an encampment I know in the Indian Mountains," replied Rowdy.

"Is that wise?" asked Frank, remembering again the stories he had heard about the area.

"The Indians won't bother us, the chief medicine man was a good friend of my father," said Rowdy quietly. "As long as you stay with me, you will be quite safe."

They camped that night deep in the clearing where Rowdy had last met his father. They dined by an open camp-fire on game shot by Jed Pickett. It had been a long time since Kital had entertained so many in his lodge. He saw before him men who were united only by their hatred for their enemy. Could the son of his former best friend unite them into a force capable of overcoming the Lazy K? Kital listened carefully, but as was his way, said nothing.

"How many men do you suppose the Lazy K can muster?" asked Bob.

"From the numbers that passed through the staging-post, I'd say too many, though we have accounted for quite a few."

"So we can reckon about forty guns," calculated his son.

"But at least they are split across the three ranches. If we had enough ammunition it shouldn't be impossible to take out each ranch separately, especially seeing the calibre of some of the men we have here," said Bob Denton looking hard at the brothers.

"What do you mean by that?" asked Frank quietly.

"Nothing, except you can obviously handle yourself pretty well. Jed tells me he fought with Rowdy and we have three cavalry troopers with a score to settle."

"And what about you, Bob?" asked Rowdy.

"I'm a deputy US marshal. I'm on the track of two outlaws, believed to be heading towards the Wastelands."

"Have you found any sign of them?" asked Frank quietly, his hand hovering over his Remington six-gun.

"Maybe; but I recognized the man who led the attack on us at Triple Creek," said Bob avoiding the question further. "Warlock Sims is a renegade wanted for murder, robbery and torture. There's a three thousand dollar reward out for him, dead or alive. So I'm going to go after him first. Anybody who helps can share the reward between them."

"Count me in," said Jed. "I need the money for my baby daughter. I came to get my own back on the Union, all I've done so far is rescue three Yankee troopers!"

"The war is long over, Jed. Now the marshal and I need all the help we can get," said Rowdy looking at the brothers.

"Always willing to help the law," said Frank's brother. He smiled as he spoke, but his voice was as cold as ice. "But what about you, Rowdy? How come the sergeant addressed you as major?"

"Because that's the position I now hold in the United States Cavalry. If that's a problem to anybody here, then now is the time to say," said Rowdy.

Rowdy looked hard at the brothers and Jed. Though he looked decidedly uncomfortable Jed said nothing. Nor did the brothers.

"Very well, gentlemen, let's turn in," continued Rowdy. "We need to get ammunition before we can do anything. So it's an early start tomorrow. We have to go back to Triple Creek and be away again before daybreak."

An hour before dawn two dark shapes moved silently towards the barn. The sole sentry, unaware of the raiders' attack on the Running Dog ranch, or the fight at Devil's Canyon, carelessly lit another cigarette. He moved casually around the area he was supposed to patrol. Expecting to see nothing, he saw nothing. Rowdy and Jed easily slipped by him into the barn. That was the easy part, getting out again loaded down with heavy ammunition was going to be a lot harder.

Rowdy had chosen Jed to accompany him for that reason. The huge Southerner was hardly the ideal man to sneak anywhere unobserved but his strength would be invaluable in carrying the ammunition back to the horses.

The interior of the barn was inky black and Rowdy could only grope around in the darkness until he found the ammunition. To his relief it was still there, under a pile of straw. However, in spite of Jed's strength it soon became obvious that they could not carry all the ammunition they needed in one trip. Heavily weighed down, they crawled slowly back to the horses. Clem, the young Handy boy, had been given the task of minding them. He waited impatiently for Rowdy and Jed to return.

It seemed to the young Handy that they had been gone forever, but only thirty minutes elapsed before they returned. They moved so quietly that they were on him before he knew it. Silently, he helped them load the ammunition on to the horses. Then Rowdy and Jed returned to the ranch.

Morning was approaching, but the moon still held sway as it flitted in and out of the clouds. Quickly and silently, they made their way back. This time their stealth was to no avail. Although they both slipped by the guard, Jed was seen by someone far more deadly.

After they passed the guard, Jed and Rowdy split up, only Jed returning to the barn. As he crossed the courtyard, the moon briefly flitted out of the clouds. For a few seconds, moonlight bathed the courtyard. Then it was gone, hidden behind more clouds. Jed froze, waiting for the cry that would mean he had been detected. None came. Jed remained motionless; experience had taught him never to move until he was sure it was safe to do so.

While Jed was making his way to the barn, Rowdy went to see if he could get his pack-mule from the corral. Angus made that task impossible. No matter how he tried to coax his pack-mule from the corral, the mule stubbornly refused to leave Angus. Seeing the great beast becoming more and more agitated, Rowdy gave up the attempt. Instead, he headed towards the barn.

As he reached the back of it, all hell broke out.

★ ★ ★

It was a little before dawn when Warlock Sims awoke. Immediately he felt for his Bowie knife. To hell with Major Norton, he was going to have one of the girls. Then he swore in frustration as he remembered that they had left with Rex Morden the previous day. He crossed to the window to check on the guard. As he did so, the moon briefly illuminated the yard and Sims saw a shadow of a huge man moving by the barn. He forgot the girls and stuffed his six-gun into his sash. As he had hoped, they had come back for the ammunition. He had found boxes of it in the barn, hidden in the straw. However, he had not told his men. Instead, he had left it as bait. He stroked the blade of his Bowie knife. To his perverted mind, this was going to be fun. Soundlessly, he left the ranch house and headed to the barn. Years of being on the run had taught Sims how to move swiftly without being detected. In spite of Jed's vigilance, the big Southerner failed to either see or hear him.

Finally, but only when he thought it safe to do so, Jed Pickett continued on his way to the barn. Speed was now as important as stealth for daybreak could not be that far away. He moved as quickly as he could in the inky darkness of the barn. Suddenly, without warning, he felt an agonizing pain in his belly. It grew worse as the big Bowie knife twisted round in his gut, again and again. Then it was gone, as suddenly as it had been plunged into him.

Screaming in agony, Jed crashed to the ground. As he did so, a lantern suddenly lit the interior of the barn. Only barely conscious, Jed saw his tormentor standing over him, lantern held aloft, blood dripping from the Bowie knife in the man's other hand. Jed could only watch as the knife came down and struck him again and again. Each blow designed to inflict the maximum amount of pain, rather than kill. Jed heard himself scream again, but Sims only laughed and continued to attack remorselessly. The inhuman laughter was the last sound that Jed heard as he fell into merciful oblivion from which he was never destined to awake.

Hearing the screams, Rowdy froze, safe for the moment in the shadow of the barn. As the screams continued, pandemonium broke out in the bunkhouse. One after the other, half-dressed gunmen poured out of it. One paused for a moment to curse at the guard who had remained at his post in spite of the screams and peals of maniacal laughter. Several of the gunmen raced towards the barn, Colts drawn. They found a blood-soaked Warlock Sims, still continuing his frenzied attack on Jed's lifeless body. It took two of the biggest gunmen to pull Sims off the corpse. By the time they had done so, they too were covered in blood. A third gunman, the one who had cursed the guard, looked down at the mutilated remains of Jed's body and rushed outside. He was violently sick. His vomit splashed on to his already bloodstained boots. The guard was less than sympathetic and mocked him.

"When you've ridden as long as I have with Colonel Sims you learn not to rush headlong into things that don't concern you. Leastways, not unless you've got a cast-iron belly."

There was nothing that Rowdy could do for Jed. Indeed his own position was becoming perilous. As gunmen swarmed round the front of the barn, the first rays of the early morning sun were already glinting on its newly white-washed walls. It would only be a few moments before the courtyard was bathed in sunlight exposing Rowdy's hiding-place.

Taking advantage of the confusion at the front of the barn, Rowdy raced back to Clem and the horses. His heart pounded furiously. At every stride he expected to hear the shout that would mean he had been discovered and feel a bullet thud into his back. None came and he reached the horses safely.

* * *

Two hours later Rowdy was back at the camp-site. After the horses had been unloaded and rubbed down, he related Jed Pickett's grisly end to the rest of the raiders. Though used to it, they were shocked by the manner of Jed's death. Over a late breakfast, Frank voiced their unspoken anger.

"Time to hit back, and hit hard. No more games. We've all lost kin and friends because of this Norton. He may not have pulled the trigger but he's the one behind their deaths."

"Very well, no quarter shall be the way of it," replied Rowdy. "After we've finished eating, sort out what ammunition you need. It's time for the raiders to ride in earnest. From now on we shoot first and do whatever it takes to defeat Norton."

"That's the second most sensible thing I've heard said today," said Frank's brother looking hard at Bob. "Let's get to it."

* * *

The attack on Triple Creek began at dusk. Dressed in civilian clothes Sergeant Browne and the two remaining troopers rode slowly up to the ranch.

"Hello the house," called Sergeant Browne, his voice sounding a good deal calmer than he actually felt.

"What can we do for you stranger?" asked the gunman who had been on guard duty the previous night. His manner seemed friendly enough but it was false.

Several gunmen came out of the bunkhouse. They moved about with an air of feigned indifference although their hands never moved far away from their six-guns. Browne also noticed that there was no sign of the two captive girls or the man they called Warlock Sims.

"Just a courtesy call," said the sergeant. "We're waiting to meet up with some friends, so we've camped nearby in the hills. We thought it only right that we should ride over and tell you. Nothing for you to worry about. We should be on our way in a day or so."

"Can I ask where you're heading, friend?" asked the gunman.

Sergeant Browne's answer was interrupted by the arrival of a very old and decrepit covered wagon, driven by an even older-looking Indian. The arrival of the wagon seemed to confuse the sergeant, who dropped one of his gauntlets. He dismounted to retrieve it.

"What do you want, Indian?" snarled the gunman. "Be off! I thought you'd have learnt your lesson in town last time we met. This ain't your home any more. You and your old wagon ain't welcome here."

They were the last words he said because, in picking up his gauntlet, the sergeant gave the prearranged signal to attack. The side of the wagon flew open, followed by a barrage of shots. Kital grabbed the carbine by his side. His first shot struck the gunman in the chest penetrating his heart. Kital had kept his word, the first of the gunmen who had pistol-whipped him in Clearwater was dead. He would scalp him later.

The other gunmen fared no better and were struck down by shots from the wagon before they could even draw. The sergeant drew his massive dragoon pistol, kicked open the ranch-house door, then charged inside. The two troopers followed close behind him. The noise of the old dragoon blasting away disturbed Angus. The mighty bull galloped towards the mules at the end of the corral furthest away from the ranch house.

Two more gunmen died as they tried

their luck against the huge dragoon pistol. All but one of the gunmen in the bunkhouse were rounded up without further fight. He fled across the corral. Rowdy took aim but could not bring himself to shoot the man in the back. It made little difference. In his haste to escape, the gunman ran straight towards the mules. Angus thinking that his friends were in danger charged at the fleeing gunman. Too late the man saw the danger. He fired his pistol at Angus, but the bullets had no effect. The gunman turned away as the mighty bull charged. Again he was too late. Angus viciously drove one of his large horns into the gunman, snapping his backbone like a twig.

It was all over in seconds. Six gunmen lay dead. The raiders had recaptured Triple Creek without so much as a scratch. However, when Sergeant Browne came out of the ranch house he could only confirm the absence of Dawn and Anne. Nor was there any sign of Warlock Sims.

Kital and Clem Hardy were delegated to supervise the burial of the dead by the prisoners. Later the raiders began to interrogate one of the gunmen. Rowdy had met him before. He was called Larry, and was the other gunman who had pistol-whipped Kital. Now he stood in the middle of the dining-room surrounded by the raiders, his eyes never leaving the fresh scalp dangling from Kital's waistband.

"They took the women to the Lazy K," Larry finally admitted.

"Who took them?" asked Rowdy.

"Rex Morden. Morden wouldn't leave them in the colonel's care. After he killed the prowler in the barn, the colonel said he was going to the Lazy K to get our money. Damn that madman! If he hadn't butchered that prowler, we might have found out about your plans to attack us."

"You should have left town when Rowdy made you and your partner strip to your long-johns," said Frank. "I heard him warn you."

"My partner is dead. The Indian did for him. What are you going to do with me?" asked Larry.

"Turn you over to the Indian, unless you can give us some reason not to," said Frank's brother.

"I could take you down the back trail to the Lazy K," said Larry.

"Through Pines Bluff? I know the trail well, I was born here. No, you've got to do better than that," said Rowdy.

"If you take me with you, I can show you where the guards are. We can even ride right up to them; they won't suspect anything if you pretend to be my prisoner. In return, all I ask is to be set free after that. I won't stop until I reach Dodge, that's for sure."

Larry was locked up with the rest of the prisoners and a council of war was held. It was decided that the Handys should remain at Triple Creek to guard the prisoners. Bob, Sergeant Browne and the two surviving troopers were to go to the Running Dog ranch and keep them pinned down by sniper fire. Rowdy, pretending to be a prisoner would go to the Lazy K. Frank and his brother would accompany him, playing the part of outlaws who wanted to meet Major Norton; roles near to their true situation. Larry would go as far as Pines Bluff but once the guards had been eliminated, Rowdy agreed to set him free. There was no mention of Kital. It was assumed that the old Indian would stay at Triple Creek.

One of the raiders had different plans for Kital. Although Rowdy had tried to cover everything, Frank's brother was not satisfied. However, he said nothing. Instead he offered to help Kital prepare supper in the kitchen. Actually, he spent most of the time deep in discussion with Kital, the outcome of which he kept to himself. He had been a wanted man for many years and trusted nobody, not even his own brother, in this particular matter.

An hour before dawn, the raiders set off. Bob and the troopers rode to the Running Dog ranch. Rowdy, pretending to be a prisoner, led Larry towards Pines Bluff, Frank and his brother followed closely behind, their handguns at the ready. Rowdy hid his special Le Mat pistol in the folds of his Texicana saddle. For appearances Larry retained his Colt but it was unloaded. Casually they rode up to the three riders guarding the trail at Pines Bluff.

"You're on the move early, Larry, who's that with you?" asked one of the gunmen drawing his six-gun.

"Easy, Tom. You're jumpy today. This is Rowdy Carter, no less," said Larry, waving his empty Colt in Rowdy's direction.

"What about the other two?" asked the first gunman.

"Old friends of mine," replied Larry. "Seems they were taking a little vacation in the mountains to get away from a troop of soldiers. By chance they ran into Carter and caught him. They were just going to string him up when I happened on the scene. I persuaded them it might be worth big money if they let me bring Carter to the major."

It was a thin story, full of holes. However, the guards bought it without question, thereby sealing their fate.

"The major will be pleased to have Carter. So will some of the boys after the trouble he's caused them," said one of the guards.

He relaxed and reholstered his six-gun. He began to smile as he thought of the mirth caused by the arrival of the three naked gunmen at the Lazy K. Since then, the luckless gunmen had been the butt of much crude humour. They would be more than pleased to give Rowdy Carter a very hot welcome.

Larry prodded Black Bart and the great stallion trotted gently forward as if he knew the role he must play in the charade. Rowdy's hands were loosely tied to the pommel of his saddle, so he guided Black Bart with his knees. The others followed and soon they passed out of sight of the gunman. They were all unaware that the whole masquerade had been observed from a dense clump of pine trees.

Although on foot, Kital had found little difficulty in keeping pace with the raiders. Undetected, he watched them ride slowly out of sight. Silently, he reached for his bow. He shared the view of Frank's brother, the guards could not be left to cut off the raiders' escape route. Besides they were the enemy. The death of his lifelong friend, John Carter could not go unavenged. That was the code of the Running Dog Indians.

Two miles further down the trail, Rowdy released Larry. The captured gunman couldn't believe that Rowdy had kept his word. Even so he had no intention of keeping his. As soon as he had ridden safely out of sight, he turned his horse round and headed for Pines Bluff. He intended to contact the guards and together they would attack the unsuspecting raiders from behind.

Then they could take the bodies to the major. He would be delighted and would reward him handsomely. As he rode into Pines Bluff, Larry burst out laughing. The day was turning out better than he had dared to hope.

Larry was still laughing when the arrow struck him in the chest; its force knocked him off his horse. He lay on the trail only semi-conscious. Suddenly, a shadow fell over him. He looked up to see Kital standing over him. Dangling from a belt round his waist were three fresh scalps. In the Indian's right hand was a tomahawk. He raised it and prepared to strike. Helpless, Larry watched the tomahawk fall towards him. The last thing he remembered was the blood already on its blade.

12

AN hour before dawn, at exactly the same time as the raiders left Triple Creek, Major Norton and Helen drove quietly out of Clearwater in a buckboard. On the back of the buckboard was a trunk. Though it was large, the trunk contained only a small selection of her clothes. The rest were still at Triple Creek.

The major had enjoyed hours of unbridled passion in Helen's bed. At the height of his passion, rather than make love, he boasted to her about his plans to overrun Triple Creek, then amalgamate the Running Dog and Lazy K ranches. He even told her of his plans to eventually become governor. Helen was impressed, though not by his lack of love-making. The latter did not stop her from accepting his invitation to stay with him at the Lazy K for as long as she lived. However, the major did not intend that to be for much longer, just a few more days until Sims secured Triple Creek and disposed of its occupants. Until then he intended to enjoy her warm and willing body.

Because of his decision to eventually dispose of Helen, the major had not wanted to be seen leaving Clearwater with her, hence their early departure. Helen, confident of her sexual prowess and the hold that it gave her over the major, agreed to the early start provided he promised to get the rest of her clothes from Triple Creek as soon as possible.

The major had expected the occupation of Triple Creek to take several days, so he was surprised to learn that Sims had accomplished it so quickly. He was especially pleased to discover that Rex Morden had insisted that the two women captives were brought to the Lazy K unharmed. He escorted Helen to the bedroom and left her to change and unpack. While she was so occupied, he sent for Sims. The outlaw was not in the best of moods at being disturbed so early and was abnormally frustrated at having to restrain his sexual desire. Realizing he had no chance of getting Dawn, Sims changed his target.

"Major, let me have the Lattimer girl; I've always fancied having a schoolteacher."

"No. I might need her to help persuade the Carter brat to sign over the water-rights," replied the major.

"Let me have the Carter girl, then. After a couple of hours with me she will be only too glad to sign whatever you want," said Sims.

Major Norton frowned. After only a couple of minutes with Sims, Dawn would be in no condition to sign anything. He could give Anne Lattimer to Sims to keep him quiet, but he might want to use Anne to get what he wanted from Dawn. The outlaw was becoming dangerously unstable but getting rid of him was going to be difficult. Sims' madness made him all the more dangerous to cross.

At that moment, the answer to Major Norton's problem entered the room. Helen had finished unpacking and although it was barely breakfast-time, she had changed into one of her most daring gowns. The major almost laughed out loud, it seemed fate had played into his hands. He saw Warlock Sims gloating at Helen, his lips drooling as he stared at the extremely low neckline of her scarlet dress. The major decided to let the man's foul nature run its unnatural course, thereby killing two birds with one stone. After Sims had disposed of Helen, ways could be found to incriminate him. Then the law, in the shape of Rex Morden, could take care of Sims. After all, he paid Morden to clear up his dirty work. Major Norton began to put his plan into action.

"Hello, my dear," he said, "you look stunning. I don't think you've met my right-hand man, Colonel Sims, have you? You remember I told you that we were going to take over the Triple Creek soon; well, Warlock has already done it."

"Well done, Colonel," said Helen smiling sexily at him. Her expression changed to a frown as she turned to speak to the major. "Darling, does that mean I can have the rest of my clothes from Triple Creek soon?"

"Warlock, I wonder if you'd do me a big favour?" asked the major.

"Depends," replied the gunman, his eyes riveted on Helen.

"Unfortunately I've some urgent business to attend to, so would you mind taking Helen back to Triple Creek for me?"

The thought of being alone on the trail with Helen filled Sims with glee. He knew that she was the major's lover and that made her even more desirable. Perhaps he could lure her away from the main trail to a place where there would be nobody to say no, except Helen, and she didn't count. He could almost hear her screams for help. Sims pulled himself together as he tried to seem uninterested, though he didn't fool the major for a second.

"Of course, Major," replied the outlaw.

"Thanks, Warlock. I think you'd better take the buckboard. I guess that Helen will have trunks full of clothes to collect."

They started out immediately without waiting for breakfast. Norton had been a poor lover, leaving Helen unsatisfied. Something in the way Sims looked at her suggested he would remedy that, given the chance. So, when he suggested a detour to a secluded wooded copse, barely visible from the trail she readily agreed. When he asked her to dismount she also agreed, then raised no objections as he started to disrobe her. Slowly and tenderly Sims removed her clothing. So slowly that she closed her eyes as she sank to the ground, naked and consumed with passion.

She didn't see the crazed look that began to cloud Sims' eyes or the Bowie knife in his hand. She screamed as it sank into her soft body, but far away from the trail there was no one to hear her. She struggled with all her might but she was no match for the madman. Again and again the knife cut into her until she ceased to struggle. Yet Sims continued to molest her. Finally, exhausted, he sank down by the mutilated remains of her once beautiful body and fell asleep.

His dreams were not about Helen, they were about the long, black hair of Anne and her beautiful white body. He slept barely an hour and awoke feeling no remorse for his terrible actions. He was incapable of such feelings. He left Helen's mutilated body where it lay and decided to return to the Lazy K. Still consumed by perverted passion he was virtually insane. Anne was his next target and he intended to deal with her in the same way as he had dealt with Helen, not just because she was attractive, but because the major had said that he could not have her and he knew that Rex Morden also wanted her.

13

THE major watched Sims drive the buckboard out of the courtyard. He was pleased with himself. He felt no remorse about the dire fate that would soon befall Helen. She knew too much about him and his past; besides, he was becoming a powerful as well as a wealthy man. There would be plenty of time for women after he had become governor. To do that he needed the power base of the combined ranches of Lazy K and Running Dog. However, the Running Dog ranch depended on the water supply from Triple Creek so he had to acquire its water-rights. The ranch itself was too small to bother with. He would return it to Dawn once she had signed over its water-rights. If Carter was still alive he could contest the validity of Dawn's actions in court. It wouldn't do him any good because, as governor, the major planned to have the courts under his control. Rex Morden entered and the major dismissed his future plans and Helen's fate from his mind. After a few minutes' discussion with his top gun, the major began to issue instructions.

"Rex, fetch me the men who came back naked from Triple Creek and then bring in the two girls."

Five minutes later they were all assembled in the big dining-room of the Lazy K. The major puffed contentedly at his cigar and allowed the tension to build up. He was enjoying himself too much to end this game too quickly. But it was no game for Dawn and Anne. So far no harm had come to them although their dresses were more than a little dishevelled. However, both were secretly delighted to learn of Sims' departure. The mood didn't last long, their joy was soon dashed by the major.

"Rex, I think you will agree that I've

been patient, very patient. As indeed have you."

"Yes, Major," replied the gunslinger dutifully.

"Well, I think our guests need to be taught a lesson in manners."

"I won't sign over the water-rights, whatever you do to me," said Dawn defiantly.

"My dear, I'm not going to do anything to you. Unlike Warlock Sims I'm not a savage. So, I'll give you a choice: sign over the water-rights of the ranch, then you and Anne are free to go. You can live in Anne's cottage until I've finished with your ranch. When I have, you can move back into it. While you're in town our new sheriff will look after you personally."

"Only too glad to," chuckled Rex.

"Never," said Dawn.

"Well now, I thought you might say that, so I had some of my men come in here. You remember the last time you met them, you made them strip at gun point? That wasn't very ladylike, was it?"

Dawn said nothing. The major paused for effect. He lit another cigar and poured himself a large whiskey before continuing. The assembled gunmen began to grin as they guessed what was coming, but they were only half right.

"You see my boys were very embarrassed, so I think that it's only right that the deed be repaid in kind."

Dawn paled though it was no more than she expected. The gunmen began to laugh, filled with expectation. Major Norton saw the expression on her face, smiled, then shook his head.

"Oh no, Dawn, not you. Rex will strip Anne! The rest of my boys can watch him do it. They can take it in turn to have their fun when Rex has finished with her while you watch. Of course, if you sign the water-rights over to me, Anne will not be touched. On that you have my word."

Dawn grabbed the papers and signed all of them. Anne was her closest and dearest friend, so she could not let the major's men get their hands on her. The major picked up the papers and smiled contentedly but he was not finished with his prisoners. He had to keep his men happy. He ordered Anne's hands to be bound, then both girls were unceremoniously dragged into the courtyard.

"But you said that if I signed the papers you would not touch Anne," protested Dawn.

"Yes, so I did," agreed Major Norton, "but I made no such promise about you, Dawn. As soon as the rest of my men are ready, you will strip or I'll have Rex shoot Anne. After my boys have had their fun, you can ride back to Clearwater, naked like you made my men. Rex will escort you and Anne to make sure that you get there. It will give the townsfolk a real treat to see you. But I always keep my word, as long as you co-operate and perform willingly, nobody will touch Anne."

Confident that his victory over Triple Creek was complete, the major gave the order for all of his men to assemble in the courtyard in front of the hacienda. They did so eagerly. They had been cooped up on the Lazy K for an age, so the dubious delights of Clearwater's whorehouse seemed like a distant memory. All thoughts of guarding the approaches to the Lazy K disappeared as Dawn began to slowly disrobe. As she began to strip the raiders approached the Lazy K, unnoticed.

Rowdy could not believe their luck. Not only were there no guards but all the activity on the Lazy K seemed to be concentrated in the courtyard. It seemed to be too good to be true, they were going to arrive undetected. Rowdy retrieved his Le Mat from under his saddle, then dismounted. Frank and his brother did likewise. Frank, too, used a Le Mat, but his brother preferred his more orthodox Navy Colt. Guns drawn, they followed Rowdy through the main entrance. Still there was no challenge.

As they walked past the outbuildings they heard a roar of approval and lurid shouts. Together the three turned in to the courtyard of the hacienda-style ranch. The two brothers fanned out on either side of Rowdy. Nobody noticed, all eyes were focused on the drama taking place in the middle of the courtyard. History, it seemed to Rowdy, was repeating itself. The reason for the lack of guards became only too apparent. Dawn stood, more than half naked, in the centre of the courtyard. It seemed that most of the Lazy K's gunmen stood around her, eagerly urging her to take off the rest of her clothes. Standing in the doorway of the hacienda was Major Norton. Next to him with her hands tied behind her back was Anne. There were tears in her eyes.

"Dawn, we must stop meeting like this," Rowdy called out.

For ten seconds there was total silence and nobody moved. It was as if the scene was etched in stone. Then all hell broke out as the gunmen flew into action. The nearest to Rowdy drew his gun but he was dead before he fired, Frank's first shot smashing into the centre of his chest. Rowdy's shot was no less accurate. Frank's brother was even more deadly, three gunmen falling to his rapid fire.

Barely thirty seconds after it started, the battle of the Lazy K was over. Dead gunmen lay strewn across the courtyard. The few who survived the raiders' onslaught threw down their weapons and surrendered. Such was the accuracy of the raiders' fire, that neither they nor Dawn were harmed.

Anne was less fortunate. Major Norton dragged her by her long, black hair into the hacienda. Frank's brother followed them. He had a score to settle with the major, family honour to be avenged. From the interior of the hacienda came Anne's piercing scream.

It was followed by a single shot, then silence.

As his brother followed the major and Anne into the hacienda, Frank sped into the nearest outbuilding looking for Sims and Morden. Still trembling, Dawn began to pick up her clothes. Rowdy holstered his Le Mat and began to help her. As he did so Rex Morden stepped out of the bunkhouse. There was a smile of derision on his face.

"Well, Johnny Reb, didn't I tell you that I'd kill you next time we met?"

"You can try," said Rowdy, moving away from Dawn.

"Oh! I think I'll do more than that. You see while I was in the bunkhouse I counted your shots. You've had six and you haven't reloaded yet. You ought to have learnt to count. Now I'm gonna count to two, then draw. Say goodbye to your stepbrother, Dawn."

On the count of two, still smiling, Morden drew. He was fast but Rowdy was faster, even using the bulky Le Mat. Not that it mattered to Morden for he was sure that he had counted Rowdy's shots correctly. The smile on Morden's face changed to an expression of disbelief as the .42 calibre bullet thudded into his chest. He stayed on his feet but his six-gun fell to the ground as his hand went to his chest in a vain attempt to staunch the flow of blood.

"Two things you should know about the Le Mat pistol," said Rowdy. "The first is that it holds nine bullets, the second is that the centre barrel . . . "

Rowdy broke off in mid-sentence. Although Morden was still on his feet it was plain that Rowdy was talking to a dead man. Yet Rowdy felt little satisfaction as Morden slowly crumpled to the ground.

Meanwhile, Frank found nobody in the first outbuilding. In the second he came face to face with Warlock Sims. Still crazed with lust, Sims had returned to the Lazy K to wait for the chance to catch Anne on her own and deal with her in the same way as he had dealt with Helen. The phoney colonel's blue uniform was covered in her blood but Frank had no way of knowing whose blood it was. He incorrectly assumed that it was Jed Pickett's. Sims' words only served to confirm his assumption, wrong though it was.

"Another damned rebel," swore Sims. "Well, this sure is my lucky day. After I've shot you, I'm gonna skin you with my Bowie knife, just like I did the last one."

Frank knew that Sims was fast. The twin-barrelled Le Mat was a bulky weapon, but he had chosen to use it rather than his Remington. The Le Mat was a rare and unique weapon with two unusual features. Morden had discovered too late that it carried nine bullets, but its other speciality was the reason Frank had chosen to use it against the insane Sims.

"Any time you're ready," said Frank, his voice ice cold.

Sims' hand dived towards the front-facing butt of his six-gun. Fast as he was, Frank was faster still. However, Frank had to cock the Le Mat to fire its central barrel. Sims fired almost simultaneously with the Le Mat. Frank felt a searing pain as the bullet cut through his side. An unholy scream rent the air as the Let Mat exploded into life. The full force of the buckshot from its central barrel blasted Sims in the face, smashing him to the floor. That was the Le Mat's other secret. Its wider central barrel carried a charge of buckshot, not bullets, making it a devastating weapon at close quarters.

Frank looked down at what was left of Warlock Sims. Most of his face had been blown away. Blood seeped from a myriad of flesh wounds in what was left of his face. Though ghastly in appearance, the wounds were not fatal. Frank walked away, leaving the madman writhing in agony on the floor, letting what was left of Sims live was payment for the way he had butchered Jed Pickett. Death was too good for the phoney colonel.

After he was sure that Frank had gone, Sims dragged himself to the buckboard, half feeling and half seeing his way. Every movement brought him agonizing pain. Slowly and painfully, he climbed into it. Without waiting for orders, the horse automatically set off at a trot. The bumpy ground caused the buckboard to jolt violently. Semiconscious, Sims moaned in agony. Between the agonizing bouts of pain, Sims swore that, if he lived, one day he would return and exact full revenge on those who had caused his suffering.

Frank returned to the courtyard in time to see his brother dragging the lifeless body of Major Norton out of the hacienda. Anne though shocked was unharmed. Frank was led into the hacienda where Dawn bathed then bandaged his wound. The bullet had cut cleanly through his side between his ribs without causing any lasting damage.

Later that afternoon they delivered the grisly cargo of corpses to Clearwater's undertaker and locked up the prisoners in jail. Anne and Dawn insisted on returning to Triple Creek while the raiders rode to the Running Dog ranch. On the way they met up with Kital. When they arrived they found that Bob and the troopers' accurate sniping had kept the remaining gunmen pinned down. They had no stomach for a fight and surrendered as soon as they learnt of the death of Major Norton. The freshly cut scalps dangling from Kital's waist may have hastened their decision.

The next two weeks were busy ones for Rowdy and Bob. However, Bob found himself spending more and more time with Anne even though he was kept busy re-establishing law and order in Clearwater. He also worked out the reward for the dead and captured gunmen. Those who had survived were held in Clearwater's jail waiting for the visit of the circuit judge, a man not noted for his leniency.

At least the forthcoming trial gave

Rowdy a sound reason to delay his departure. He spent most of the time with Dawn. He had grown to care for her a great deal and she seemed to enjoy his company, too much for their own good. Rowdy had come to realize that his feelings towards his stepsister were far from brotherly, but did his best to keep them to himself. Apart from any other reason, his life in the cavalry would be full of danger and hardship. It was a life he would never ask any woman to share. Besides, someone had to run Triple Creek. Whatever Dawn's true feelings were, she kept them to herself. Even so, it was clear that she welcomed every precious minute she spent with Rowdy.

After the trial was over Frank and his brother became ever more restless. Rowdy too had no further excuse to stay and reluctantly made his preparations to leave for Fort Smith. The raiders met up for the last time in the main street of Clearwater.

"Time to move on. Unless you have any objections, Marshal?" asked Frank.

"None. As far as I'm concerned, you and your brother are free to come and go as you please, but what about the reward money?"

"Whatever else you've heard about us, we don't touch blood money. Send it to Jed Pickett's little girl," replied Frank's brother.

Bob and Rowdy said their goodbyes to Frank and his brother and watched them as they rode off down the main street. Resplendent in his new major's uniform and plumed hat, Rowdy mounted Black Bart. The ugly stallion was only too eager to get away from Clearwater and that great hairy beast they called Angus, even though it meant leaving his friend the pack-mule behind. Angus seemed to have adopted him but the stallion was not about to object. Rowdy was about to join Sergeant Browne and the two troopers as they cantered down the main street, when Bob interrupted him.

"You know I never did get round to asking the name of Frank's brother," said Bob.

"Me neither," grinned Rowdy, "but then I always did figure that too much of the wrong information ain't good for your health."

So saying, Rowdy whirled Black Bart round and galloped after the troopers. He didn't look back; there was no point, it would be years before he would be able to return.

THE END

TOP HAND
Wade Everett

The Broken T was big. But no ranch is big enough to let a man hide from himself.

GUN WOLVES OF LOBO BASIN
Lee Floren

The Feud was a blood debt. When Smoke Talbot found the outlaws who gunned down his folks he aimed to nail their hide to the barn door.

SHOTGUN SHARKEY
Marshall Grover

The westbound coach carrying the indomitable Larry and Stretch headed for a shooting showdown.

FIGHTING RAMROD
Charles N. Heckelmann

Most men would have cut their losses, but Frazer counted the bullets in his guns and said he'd soak the range in blood before he'd give up another inch of what was his.

LONE GUN
Eric Allen

Smoke Blackbird had been away too long. The Lequires had seized the Blackbird farm, forcing the Indians and settlers off, and no one seemed willing to fight! He had to fight alone.

THE THIRD RIDER
Barry Cord

Mel Rawlins wasn't going to let anything stand in his way. His father was murdered, his two brothers gone. Now Mel rode for vengeance.

ARIZONA DRIFTERS
W. C. Tuttle

When drifting Dutton and Lonnie Steelman decide to become partners they find that they have a common enemy in the formidable Thurston brothers.

TOMBSTONE
Matt Braun

Wells Fargo paid Luke Starbuck to outgun the silver-thieving stagecoach gang at Tombstone. Before long Luke can see the only thing bearing fruit in this eldorado will be the gallows tree.

HIGH BORDER RIDERS
Lee Floren

Buckshot McKee and Tortilla Joe cut the trail of a border tough who was running Mexican beef into Texas. They stopped the smuggler in his tracks.

BRETT RANDALL, GAMBLER
E. B. Mann

Larry Day had the choice of running away from the law or of assuming a dead man's place. No matter what he decided he was bound to end up dead.

THE GUNSHARP
William R. Cox

The Eggerleys weren't very smart. They trained their sights on Will Carney and Arizona's biggest blood bath began.

THE DEPUTY OF SAN RIANO
Lawrence A. Keating and
Al. P. Nelson

When a man fell dead from his horse, Ed Grant was spotted riding away from the scene. The deputy sheriff rode out after him and came up against everything from gunfire to dynamite.

FARGO: MASSACRE RIVER
John Benteen

The ambushers up ahead had now blocked the road. Fargo's convoy was a jumble, a perfect target for the insurgents' weapons!

SUNDANCE: DEATH IN THE LAVA
John Benteen

The Modoc's captured the wagon train and its cargo of gold. But now the halfbreed they called Sundance was going after it . . .

HARSH RECKONING
Phil Ketchum

Five years of keeping himself alive in a brutal prison had made Brand tough and careless about who he gunned down . . .

FARGO: PANAMA GOLD
John Benteen

With foreign money behind him, Buckner was going to destroy the Panama Canal before it could be completed. Fargo's job was to stop Buckner.

FARGO:
THE SHARPSHOOTERS
John Benteen

The Canfield clan, thirty strong were raising hell in Texas. Fargo was tough enough to hold his own against the whole clan.

PISTOL LAW
Paul Evan Lehman

Lance Jones came back to Mustang for just one thing — revenge! Revenge on the people who had him thrown in jail.

HELL RIDERS
Steve Mensing

Wade Walker's kid brother, Duane, was locked up in the Silver City jail facing a rope at dawn. Wade was a ruthless outlaw, but he was smart, and he had vowed to have his brother out of jail before morning!

DESERT OF THE DAMNED
Nelson Nye

The law was after him for the murder of a marshal — a murder he didn't commit. Breen was after him for revenge — and Breen wouldn't stop at anything . . . blackmail, a frameup . . . or murder.

DAY OF THE COMANCHEROS
Steven C. Lawrence

Their very name struck terror into men's hearts — the Comancheros, a savage army of cutthroats who swept across Texas, leaving behind a bloodstained trail of robbery and murder.

SUNDANCE: SILENT ENEMY
John Benteen

A lone crazed Cheyenne was on a personal war path. They needed to pit one man against one crazed Indian. That man was Sundance.

LASSITER
Jack Slade

Lassiter wasn't the kind of man to listen to reason. Cross him once and he'll hold a grudge for years to come — if he let you live that long.

LAST STAGE TO GOMORRAH
Barry Cord

Jeff Carter, tough ex-riverboat gambler, now had himself a horse ranch that kept him free from gunfights and card games. Until Sturvesant of Wells Fargo showed up.

Doncaster
Council

DONCASTER LIBRARY AND INFORMATION SERVICES
www.doncaster.gov.uk
Please return/renew this item by the
last date shown.
Thank you for using your library.

InPress 0231 MAY 18